SELLO S. MAKHAFOLA

DAUGHTERS OF THE DARKNESS

Infinite Realms

"The world is full of magic things, patiently waiting for our senses to grow sharper."

— W.B Yeats

Contents

1

CHAPTER I — The Host.

Deep within the woods, two hunters, Calantha Singh and Ayla Blackwood, stood victorious over their latest prize. A half-human, half-wolf creature, Maverick Moonlight, lay bound and helpless within a sturdy cage. The moon cast an eerie glow over the scene as Odessa Moonstone approached, her footsteps quiet on the forest floor. "What do we have here?" Odessa asked, her eyes fixed on Maverick. "Behold, this is Maverick Moonlight," Calantha replied, a hint of pride in her voice. Odessa's gaze narrowed. "What?" — "Half-human, half-wolf," Ayla explained. "Haven't seen one of these in centuries." Calantha and Ayla began to circle the cage, their movements fluid and practiced. Odessa's eyes never left Maverick. "You said Moonlight?" Odessa asked, her tone laced with curiosity. "Yes, Moonlight," Calantha replied. "The glow of the night." Odessa's expression turned grave. "Oh, no."

Calantha and Ayla halted their pacing, sensing a shift in Odessa's demeanor. They approached her, their faces questioning. "What?" Ayla asked. "I believe this is one of mine," Odessa said, her voice low and measured. Calantha's brow furrowed. "What do you mean by one of yours?" Odessa's gaze drifted back to Maverick. "From my realm. Selenea." Ayla's confusion deepened. "Odessa, what are you on about?" Odessa's eyes locked onto hers. "The realm Selenea is named after Selene, the Greek goddess of the moon. And everyone's last name there starts with 'Moon.'" Calantha's eyes widened. "So, Moonlight and Moonstone?" Odessa nodded. Ayla's face twisted in skepticism. "So, we're releasing it?" Odessa approached the cage, her movements deliberate. "Oh, no. This is something else. Originally, we aren't half-breeds, so whatever this is… it's big and never happened before." Calantha's eyes met Ayla's, then returned to Odessa. "Okay, Odessa. What shall we do now, since we've caught one of your… kin?" Odessa's gaze never wavered. "We study it." Ayla's discontent was palpable. "I didn't leave my realm to study another creature from a different realm. We're here to hunt mortals, remember?" Odessa's voice rose, a hint of authority creeping in. "Listen! I think we should just leave it here for now and come back tomorrow." Without another word, the trio departed, leaving Maverick Moonlight alone in the heart of the woods, a pawn in a game yet to unfold.

The trio settled into their cramped, one-room apartment, the air thick with unspoken questions. Calantha and Ayla's gazes converged on Odessa, their eyes burning with curiosity. "So, what are you?" Calantha asked, her voice low and measured. "A half-breed too?" Odessa's expression remained serene. "No, I'm not." Ayla's brow furrowed. "So, Maverick just transformed into a half-wolf?" Odessa's eyes clouded, her thoughts distant. "I think maybe… something got into her body." — "Like making her a host?" Ayla pressed, her tone laced with intrigue. Odessa nodded. "Exactly. But what could've gotten into her?"

Calantha's gaze snapped back to the conversation. "Guys, isn't it obvious? A wolf probably got into her body. That's why she's half-wolf, half-human." Odessa's expression turned grave. "No, our bodies… when we were made… they designed us to be impervious. Our bodies can't be hosts to anything – not demons, nothing." Ayla's eyes sparkled with insight. "Listen, what if… hear me out… what if your sister's been in the mortal realm too long? Mortals can be unpredictable. Maybe they did something to her." Odessa's gaze lingered on Ayla, her expression thoughtful. "Perhaps you're right." Calantha's thoughts shifted to the practicalities. "You said we should study Maverick. Doesn't that require dissecting it? To see what's inside?" Odessa's voice was laced with hesitation. "I don't think we should kill her… yet." Ayla's eyes narrowed. "Yet? You're suggesting we might kill one of your own kind?" Odessa's jaw set. "If Maverick poses a threat, yes." The tension was palpable, but Calantha's voice cut through the silence. "Enough about this. It's time to hunt mortals." With that, the trio rose, their movements fluid and practiced, and slipped into the night, leaving the mystery of Maverick Moonlight temporarily unresolved.

The trio blended into the shadows, observing the mortals' revelry. Ayla's sudden transformation into a different person left Calantha and Odessa stunned. "You can shapeshift?" Calantha asked, her voice barely above a whisper. Ayla's smile was nonchalant. "Well, yes." Odessa's eyes narrowed. "How is it we only find out now?" Ayla shrugged. "Didn't seem relevant until now. How about I grab a few mortals?" Calantha and Odessa nodded, their faces set with anticipation. Ayla vanished into the crowd, leaving her sisters to wait. Inside the throng, Ayla's newfound persona drew attention. A stranger approached, his voice lost in the music. "Hey, you look beautiful. What's your name?" he yelled. Ayla cupped her ear, feigning difficulty hearing. "Uh… what?" The stranger leaned in, his breath warm against her ear. "I said, what's your name?" Ayla's smile was radiant. "Oh, I'm Ayla. What's yours?"

Their conversation flowed effortlessly, culminating in a suggestive invitation. Ayla's lips brushed against the stranger's, a fleeting kiss. Her sisters watched, amused. "Seriously?" Odessa asked, raising an eyebrow. Ayla winked. "Just wanted to feel the tangling sensation they're always yapping about."

Calantha intervened, her eyes sparkling with mischief. A sleeping spell enveloped the stranger, and they caught him as he swooned. Ayla repeated her hunt, returning with two more strangers. As they walked away, Odessa glanced back, sensing a presence in the darkness. A figure watched, hidden. "I think we should hurry," Odessa urged, her voice low and urgent. The trio quickened their pace, arriving at their apartment with their captives. Tied to chairs, the strangers seemed bewildered.

"Hunting mortals doesn't thrill me anymore," Calantha confessed. Ayla, now back in her true form, asked, "Why's that?"

Calantha's gaze turned introspective. "We're hunting mortals, only to hand them over to their own kind." Ayla countered, "The ones we're handing them over to aren't normal, remember? They're a cult." Odessa's eyes lit up. "Perhaps we can ask them about my half-breed sister." Ayla nodded, her expression resolute. "Yeah. Let's do that."

2

CHAPTER II — Shifting Allegiances.

The next day, Odessa summoned Cassius Haven, leader of the mysterious cult, to collect the mortal captives. Cassius arrived with two loyal followers, Kael Jensen and Luna Nightshade. As he inspected the bound mortals, Odessa, Ayla, and Calantha observed from a distance. "Always a pleasure doing business with you three," Cassius said, his voice dripping with sincerity. "What's the payment this time?" — "Nothing, for now," Odessa replied. "But there's something else." Cassius's curiosity was piqued. "I'm listening." Odessa's gaze drifted toward the window facing the woods. "Seeing it would make more sense."

With a nod, Cassius ordered his followers to escort the mortals back to the cult's premises. The group then ventured into the heart of the woods, where Maverick Moonlight remained caged.

Cassius's eyes widened as he took in the half-human, half-wolf creature. "Well, well. What do we have here?"

Odessa's expression turned grave. "Half-human, half-wolf. My kind isn't susceptible to hosting… whatever this is." Cassius's eyes sparkled with intrigue. "I see. Am I taking this one too?"

Odessa's voice was firm. "No, this is my sister. Whatever happened to her is terrifying." Cassius's smile was knowing. "You wanted my expertise, because I own a cult." Odessa nodded. "Exactly. My kind can't be hosts." — "If so then this might be impossible to fix." Cassius said. Calantha's frustration boiled over. "You haven't even inspected her thoroughly, and you're already concluding it's hopeless?" Cassius's tone turned condescending. "Listen, child. I've dealt with similar situations."

Calantha's anger flared, but Ayla and Odessa restrained her. "Fine," Calantha spat. "What does he even know?"

Cassius's smirk was arrogant. "I know many things. I lead the largest cult in Emberdale — The Order of the Eternal Flames."

Calantha's laughter was laced with disdain. "Eternal flames, you say?" Cassius's eyes gleamed with fanaticism. "I'm doing what your false gods can't – creating hell on earth." Odessa intervened, her voice measured. "Let's focus on why we're here."

Cassius shrugged. "Right. I won't be much help with this. Call me when you want to discuss eternal torture, screams, and pain. Those are topics I enjoy."

With that, Cassius departed, leaving the trio to ponder their next move. After a few minutes, they followed, the mystery of Maverick Moonlight's fate still unresolved.

Cassius returned to his cult's hideout, where his followers surrounded the three strangers. Ophelia approached him, her eyes gleaming with an unsettling intensity. "This doesn't bring joy like it used to," Ophelia said, her voice laced with discontent. "We need something to grab the attention of the false gods."

Cassius's chuckle sent a shiver down Ophelia's spine. "I might have something," he whispered, his eyes sparkling with malevolence. Ophelia's smile was a cold, calculated thing.

Meanwhile, in the hunters' apartment, Calantha's restlessness simmered. "I feel like we're wasting our gifts," Calantha said, her voice tinged with frustration. "Shouldn't we do something more significant?" Ayla's curiosity was piqued. "What do you suggest?" Calantha's gaze drifted, her thoughts unfocused. "I don't know… yet. But hunting mortals isn't doing it anymore." Ayla's eyes narrowed. "The cult." Calantha's attention snapped back. "What about it?" Ayla's expression turned resolute. "You heard Cassius – he wants to create hell on earth. He'll terrorize everything, bring hell to their doorstep. Why don't we help the mortals instead of hunting them down?" Odessa's eyes met Ayla's, a spark of understanding igniting. "Not a bad idea, actually," Odessa said, her voice measured. The hunters' gaze converged, their minds racing with the possibilities. The cult, once their allies, now threatened to become their enemies. The tide of their allegiance was shifting, and the consequences would be catastrophic.

Three weeks had passed since the hunters' decision to help the mortals. Odessa, Ayla, and Calantha blended into the crowd at Emberdale High, their high school uniforms a perfect disguise. As they entered the cafeteria, all eyes turned toward them. The trio claimed an empty table, their confidence undeniable. A stranger approached, his smile friendly. "Hello, ladies. I believe you're new here?" Odessa's gaze drifted to his jacket, where his name was embroidered. "You're Nicholas Grey." Nicholas chuckled, following his gaze. "Yes, I am." Calantha's invitation was laced with flirtation. "Well, sit down, Nicky." Nicholas sat, his eyes sparkling with curiosity. The hunters began to touch him, their movements slow and deliberate. Nicholas laughed, his cheeks flushing. "What are you ladies doing?" he asked, his voice tinged with amusement. Ayla's smile was playful. "Should we stop, Nicky?" Nicholas shook his head, his grin growing. "Of course not." Their playful banter drew attention. A security guard intervened, his expression stern. "No inappropriate touching, please." Odessa's smile was enigmatic, while Calantha and Ayla's gazes remained fixed on Nicholas. The guard retreated, his unease palpable. Ayla's questions flowed effortlessly. "So, Nicky, do you have a girlfriend?" Nicholas hesitated, his face reddening. Odessa leaned in, her whisper conspiratorial. "Sister, these questions… where did you get them?" Ayla's reply was barely audible. "Internet." Their conversation continued, a delicate dance of flirtation and curiosity. The hunters' intentions remained hidden, their true nature concealed behind masks of innocence.

3

CHAPTER III — The Mortal's Heart.

The next day, Cassius and his cult members arrived at the woods in their large truck, eager to claim their prize. As they stepped out, Ophelia's eyes sparkled with excitement. "This is next level," she whispered, her gaze fixed on the cage holding Maverick. "Should probably piss off a few false gods." Cassius's grin was wicked. "Who does it belong to?" Kael asked, his curiosity piqued. "Remember those three ladies who bring us mortals?" Cassius replied, his eyes glinting with malice. "It belongs to one of them, Odessa. If this will actually piss off these false gods, then next time we're taking her." The group erupted into chuckles as they loaded the cage into the truck. They fled the scene, leaving an empty space at the heart of the woods. Back at their cult's hideout, they unloaded the cage and placed it inside a dimly lit warehouse. Cassius stood before Maverick, his eyes gleaming with anticipation. "So, what do you suggest we do with it, Cassius?" Kael asked, his voice laced with curiosity. Cassius's response was immediate. "Sacrifice it, of course." Maverick raised her head for the first time since her capture, her eyes blazing with defiance. "Set…uh…me…free…"

she whispered, her voice trembling. "I shall give you all you want." Cassius's chuckle was low and menacing. "Create hell on earth, would you do that for me?" Maverick's gaze locked onto Cassius, her eyes burning with intensity. "You shall suffer my wrath," she vowed, her voice steady. "That's a promise. I'm the daughter of the great Selenea Imperia." Cassius's teasing tone turned cruel. "Oh, how sad? You got a mother? Mom's dead. Sacrificed her to start this cult." Maverick's expression remained resolute, her silence a testament to her unyielding spirit.

Cassius continued, his voice dripping with arrogance. "I used to call this cult 'The Darkfire Church of the Night,' but it didn't seem quite intimidating. So now we call it 'The Order of the Eternal Flames,' and I, Cassius, shall create hell on earth." The cult members erupted into mocking laughter, believing Maverick to be hopeless. But her eyes told a different story – one of determination and vengeance.

Meanwhile, in a bustling classroom at Emberdale High, Nicholas and the three sisters' friendship had blossomed with alarming speed. Calantha's curiosity got the better of her. "Nicky, are you afraid of monsters?" Nicholas chuckled. "Why would I be afraid of things that don't exist? They're just myths." Odessa's eyes sparkled with mischief. "What if they do exist?" Nicholas shrugged. "Well, they'll have to show themselves." With a parting smile, he left to join his friends. The sisters exchanged knowing glances. "He's so handsome," Ayla sighed, her cheeks flushing.

Calantha's expression turned stern. "Focus, sister. You can't fall in love with this mortal. You'll become vulnerable." Ayla's smile was wistful. "Mortals say that's the best thing." Calantha's tone remained cautionary. "Yes, for them, but for us, it can be dangerous." Odessa's concern shifted to her captive sister. "While we're on the topic of danger, why don't we check up on Maverick?" The trio slipped out of the classroom, navigating through the crowded hallways. They passed Nicholas and his friends, who couldn't help but stare. Upon arriving at the woods, they found an empty space – no cage, no Maverick, nothing.

Odessa's anxiety spiked. "Where is she?" Calantha's brow furrowed. "You think she managed to set herself free, left and took the cage with her?" Odessa's expression turned skeptical. "Likely impossible. Someone helped her, but who." Ayla's eyes narrowed. "What if Cassius did this?" Odessa's concern deepened. "What? All he wants is mortals. What would he do with a half-breed?" Ayla's voice was laced with unease. "Piss off the false gods, like he said." Odessa's determination hardened. "We need to go there and retrieve my sister before that monster does something he'll regret." Calantha's caution was palpable. "What if their powers are too much?" Odessa's confidence remained unwavering. "They're mortal, and we're immortal. We should be fine." Calantha's strategic mind kicked in. "But let's strategize this first." Odessa nodded, and the trio retreated to their apartment, their minds racing with the impending rescue mission.

Nicholas shot hoops with his friends, Austin and Mike, at the local basketball court. The sun began to set, casting a warm orange glow over the scene. "Nick, are you dating one of those three girls you're always with?" Mike asked, curiosity etched on his face. Nicholas chuckled. "I wish." Austin grinned. "The one with the long hair would definitely look good on you." Nicholas shrugged. "I think they've already friendzoned me." Austin raised an eyebrow. "What makes you say that?" — "They're no longer flirtatious like they used to be, especially the one with the long hair," Nicholas explained. Austin and Mike exchanged a knowing glance, their eyes drifting behind Nicholas. "Are you sure about that?" they asked in unison, nodding toward the approaching figure. Nicholas turned to find Ayla, her long hair cascading down her back like a golden waterfall. Their eyes met, and Nicholas's heart skipped a beat. A smile spreading across his face. "Hey, Ayla. Where are your sisters?" Ayla's cheeks flushed. "Hey, Nicky. I just wanted to see you… alone… so, they're back at the apartment." Nicholas's curiosity piqued. "So, they know you're here?" Ayla's laughter was music to his ears. "No. And can you not tell them, please?" Nicholas's grin turned mischievous. "Only if you come over to my place sometimes." Ayla's eyes sparkled. "Oh, Nicky." — "Is that a yes?" Nicholas asked, his voice low and hopeful. Ayla's smile was her answer. "Yes, it's a yes." — "Let's take a walk," Nicholas suggested, turning to his friends. "See you all tomorrow." Austin and Mike nodded, their faces splitting into knowing smiles. As Nicholas and Ayla strolled away from the court, the stars began to twinkle above. The air was filled with the sweet scent of blooming flowers. "So, why did you want to see me alone?" Nicholas asked, his arm brushing against Ayla's. Ayla's voice was barely above a whisper. "I've never dated a human before, so I…" Nicholas's eyes locked onto hers. "What do you mean you never dated a human before?" Ayla's cheeks flushed. "I was trying to say I never dated anyone before. That's all." Nicholas's expression softened. "Okay."

The two walked in comfortable silence, enjoying each other's company. As the night wore on, Ayla reluctantly bid Nicholas farewell, returning to the apartment. Her sisters greeted her with curious expressions. "Sister, where have you been?" Odessa asked. Ayla's smile was innocent. "Needed some air." Odessa's eyes narrowed. "But we always go out together." Ayla's voice was laced with reassurance. "I know, and it won't happen again." Odessa's gaze lingered, searching for the truth. But Ayla's secret remained hidden, locked away in her heart.

4

CHAPTER IV — Infinite Realms.

Two days had passed since Maverick's capture. The air was heavy with anticipation at the cult hideout, a foreboding sense of excitement hanging over the congregation like a dark cloud.

Cassius stood tall, his eyes blazing with fervor, as he addressed his followers. Kael, Ophelia, Aria, and Luna stood in the front row, their faces twisted with zealotry. "Behold," Cassius declared, his voice dripping with malice. "Today, we shall sacrifice these lost souls to the Eternal Flames." The congregation erupted into applause, their voices echoing through the dimly lit warehouse. But Cassius raised his hand, silencing them.

"Fixers, be still," he commanded. "I, Cassius, shall create hell on this mortal realm. No one will stop me, not even the false gods. They will tremble before our power." The congregation began to chant, their voices rising in a crescendo of fervor. "Cassius, Cassius, Cassius..."

Cassius's eyes gleamed with excitement as he continued, his words dripping with venom. "Brothers and sisters, behold the price of our salvation! These mortals give their lives so that we may rise above the weak and claim our rightful place. And I,

Cassius, shall unleash a maelstrom of darkness upon this mortal realm, forging an era of shadow and flame." With that he started slaughtering the innocent three strangers.

As he spoke, the air seemed to grow thicker, the shadows deepening and twisting around him. Suddenly, lightning began to strike, illuminating the dark warehouse with flashes of electric blue. The strikes were relentless, pounding against the earth like a drumbeat from the underworld.

The congregation's chants grew louder, their voices merging with the thunderous applause of the lightning. Cassius's eyes blazed with an otherworldly energy, his presence seeming to grow larger, more imposing. In this moment, he was the master of the universe, the bringer of darkness and chaos. And his followers were eager to unleash this hell upon the world.

Meanwhile, at the hunters' apartment, Calantha's urgent call drew her sisters outside. "Guys, come look outside," she said, her voice laced with concern. Odessa and Ayla rushed to her side, and together they gazed up at the sky. Dark, foreboding clouds had gathered, shrouding the entire horizon in an ominous gloom. "Is this one of Cassius's doings?" Odessa asked, her brow furrowed with worry. "I believe so," Ayla replied, her eyes scanning the eerie landscape. Odessa's expression turned fierce. "Let's hope he didn't kill Maverick yet, because I will dissect his body myself." Just then, a brilliant light illuminated their apartment, drawing them back inside. As they entered, they were met with a regal figure standing tall, her presence commanding attention. Selenea Imperia, the ruler of the Selenea realm, stood before them. Her piercing gaze seemed to see right through them, her majestic aura radiating an otherworldly power. Odessa, recognizing her mother, bowed down in reverence. She nudged her sisters, signaling them to follow suit. Calantha and Ayla bowed, their heads inclined in respect. "Stand up, children," the Imperia said, her voice like music. As they rose, Odessa's eyes locked onto her mother's. "Mother?" she asked, her voice barely above a whisper. The Imperia's gaze swept the room, her expression stern. "I sense chaos on this realm, and I've detected that one of my children is being held against her will." Odessa's face twisted with concern. "Yes, Mother. They're holding Maverick." The Imperia's expression turned grave. "You and your sibling, Maverick, don't belong on this mortal realm." Odessa's voice took on a pleading tone. "Forgive me, Mother, but can we save Maverick first?" A hint of a smile played on the Imperia's lips. "I could use a chair." Calantha hastened to offer her a seat, and the Imperia sat, her elegance unmistakable. The sisters followed suit, their eyes fixed on Odessa's mother. The Imperia's gaze turned to Calantha. "You're from this realm, aren't you?" Calantha nodded. "Yes, I am." Odessa's curiosity got the better of her. "You are?" she asked, her eyes narrowing. Calantha's voice was steady. "I'm a witch." The Imperia's eyes sparkled with interest. "Who do you pray to? Lucifer Morningstar?" Calantha's reply was firm. "The triple goddess— Maiden, Mother, and Crone." The Imperia's smile grew. "One could say you're one of us. Maiden represents a new moon, Mother represents a full moon, and Crone represents a waning moon." Her gaze shifted to Ayla. "And you, my dear, well… your realm has long vanished. I believe you're the last of your kind."

Odessa's eyes widened in surprise. "Wait, Mother? You know everything about everyone here?" The Imperia's response was simple. "Yes." The Imperia's piercing gaze turned to Ayla once more. "Do you know anything about your realm?" she asked, her voice dripping with curiosity. Ayla's brow furrowed, her eyes clouding with uncertainty. "No… I've always thought this mortal realm was mine too." The Imperia's expression turned thoughtful, her eyes narrowing as she examined Ayla's features. "They must have birthed you here," she mused. "But by the shape of your ears, I believe you belong to a realm called Khaosia—a realm of eternal darkness, chaos, and transformation." Odessa's eyes widened, her gaze snapping to Ayla. "Transformation?" she exclaimed. "This explains your ability to shapeshift!" Ayla's face lit up with understanding, her eyes sparkling with wonder. Odessa turned to her mother, her expression grave. "How do we save Maverick?" Calantha's voice cut in, her tone laced with concern. "Cassius's ultimate goal was to piss off the false gods." The Imperia's eyes narrowed, her gaze piercing. "So, this Cassius views us as false gods?" Odessa nodded, her jaw clenched. "He's mortal, too. Powerful, but we have no idea where he gets all his powers." The Imperia's expression turned thoughtful, her eyes glinting with calculation. "He must be worshipping someone powerful… someone celestial." Ayla's voice piped up, her eyes sparkling with insight. "Like Lucifer?" The Imperia's smile was fierce. "Exactly!" She rose from her chair, her presence commanding attention. "Since you said he wants to piss off the false gods, I shall visit him myself. Point me in the right direction." Odessa's voice was firm, her eyes locked onto her mother's. "I think we'll go with you, Mother." The Imperia's gaze swept Odessa, her expression unreadable. But a hint of approval flickered in her eyes, and she nodded.

5

CHAPTER V — Divine Intervention.

Cassius's conversation with his cult members was interrupted by the arrival of four figures: Odessa, Ayla, Calantha, and a majestic woman with an otherworldly aura. Cassius's gaze shifted from Odessa to the stranger, his eyes narrowing. "You've brought another mortal for me?" Cassius sneered, his voice dripping with malice. The Imperia's response was icy. "I am not a mortal." A loud noise echoed from the back, followed by Maverick's haunting howl. The Imperia's head snapped towards the sound, her eyes flashing with concern. "What was that?" The Imperia demanded. Cassius smirked. "Just a long-lost prisoner, nothing to worry about. I'll use her in the future." Cassius's gaze locked onto the Imperia, his expression stern. "And who are you, exactly?" The Imperia chuckled and said, "You wanted to piss off the false gods? Congratulations, you've succeeded." — "You're no god, nor a false one." Cassius said. The Imperia's eyes blazed with fury, her voice thundering. "You're holding one of mine!" She grasped Cassius by the neck, lifting him off the ground. "I AM THE RULER OF THE SELENEA REALM, AND A 'FALSE GOD' APPARENTLY!"

Calantha's spell immobilized the cult members, preventing their escape. The Imperia turned to Odessa, her voice commanding. "Go free Maverick." Odessa and Ayla hastened to Maverick's cage, their faces set with determination. Maverick's eyes locked onto Odessa's, her voice laced with a mix of sadness and understanding. "Finally, Sister. Mother got you back to your senses." Odessa's expression softened. "I wasn't going to hurt you, Maverick." Maverick's hearing, attuned to the supernatural, had picked up Odessa's earlier words. "Sister, I heard you say that if I posed a threat, I should be killed." Odessa chuckled, her eyes sparkling with relief. "I was joking, Maverick."

With Maverick freed, the Imperia released Cassius, her gaze never leaving her daughter. "Come to me, child," she said, her voice filled with warmth. Maverick's half-wolf form dissolved as she walked towards her mother. The Imperia's arms enveloped her, and Maverick's true form was restored.

The Imperia's family stood united, their bond unbreakable. With a clap of her hands, they vanished, leaving Cassius and his cult members stunned and helpless.

Back at the apartment, Odessa's curiosity got the better of her. "Why was Maverick half-human and half-wolf?" she asked, her eyes locked onto her mother's. The Imperia's expression turned somber. "Like I said, you and Maverick don't belong on this mortal realm. They must have done something to her." Maverick's gaze drifted to Calantha, her eyes clouding with memories. "Witches did that to me," she said, her voice barely above a whisper. The Imperia's gaze swept her daughters, her expression resolute. "I believe it's time we all go home."

Odessa's jaw clenched, her determination evident. "I'm sorry to ruin your trip home, but I shall remain here and protect this realm from Cassius." The Imperia's chuckle was low and husky. "From that mortal I just strangled? What danger could he possibly pose?" Odessa's eyes blazed with conviction. "He wants to create hell on earth. I can't let him do that; people will die." Maverick's voice was laced with pragmatism. "Come on, Sister. Mortals are bound to die, and they always die horrible deaths. There's nothing you can do about it." Odessa's resolve remained unshaken. "Well, I'll save them from dying early." The Imperia's expression turned stern, her voice firm. "Don't come to me looking for help when these mortals you're trying so hard to save turn on you." Odessa's eyes locked onto her mother's, her voice filled with emotion. "You're my mother." The Imperia's gaze remained unyielding. "It doesn't matter. If you decide to remain here, don't call for me." With that, she turned to Maverick. "Let's go home, Mave." Maverick's gaze met Odessa's, her eyes sparkling with a mix of sadness and understanding. "So long, Sister," she said, before she and her mother vanished into thin air, leaving Odessa with Ayla and Calantha.

The next day at Emberdale High, Ayla, Calantha, and Odessa huddled in the ladies' toilet, skipping class. Ayla's curiosity got the better of her. "So, your mother really cut you off?" Odessa's expression turned somber. "It appears so. But we can't dwell on that now. Cassius will strike soon, especially if he's worshiping the dark lord." Calantha's determination was evident. "We'll be ready for him." Odessa's gaze locked onto her friends. "Saving these mortals isn't the only reason I'm staying. I won't leave you, Ayla, after losing your realm. And Calantha, this mortal realm is yours, but I won't abandon you either." Ayla's eyes sparkled with gratitude. "Thank you, Odessa." Their conversation was interrupted by two girls, Chloe and Jasmine, who entered the toilet. Chloe's voice was laced with malice. "Ayla, stay away from Nicholas. He's mine." Odessa's eyes narrowed, her gaze flicking to their jackets. "Well, Chloe and Jasmine, you don't know who you're playing with. My sister climbs that Nicholas of yours like a mountain." Chloe's face twisted with anger. "You'll regret this."

As they walked away, Odessa called out, "Bye, Chloe. Bye, Jasmine." Calantha turned to Ayla, her brow raised. "Is there something you're not telling us, Sister?" Ayla's cheeks flushed. "I once went out alone to see Nicky." Odessa's expression was knowing. "I knew it. 'Going out for some air' was quite a story."

Ayla's voice was defensive. "I thought knowing them better would help us protect these mortals." As they exited the toilet, they bumped into Nicholas. Calantha's smile was sly. "Oh, if it isn't lovely Nicholas." Nick's eyes sparkled with warmth. "Hey, guys. Want to grab a seat together?" Calantha's tone was playful. "Nicky, stop acting weird. We know about you and Ayla – and apparently Chloe too." Nick's expression turned concerned. "What does Chloe have to do with this?" Calantha's eyes glinted with amusement. "She threatened Ayla, saying she'd regret whatever she's doing with you, Nicky." Nick's face darkened. "Chloe's crazy. There's nothing going on between us." Odessa's voice was firm. "Don't explain, Nicky. Take Ayla aside and apologize properly." Nick nodded, leading Ayla away. His words were sincere, and Ayla forgave him.

6

CHAPTER VI — Consequences of Power.

Two Days Later… Cassius stood before his cult members, his expression still haunted by the encounter with the Imperia. "I'm telling you, her eyes glowed," he insisted, his voice laced with a mix of awe and unease. "That wasn't a false god." Kael stepped forward, a sly smile spreading across his face. "Come on, Cassius. You, of all people, should know better. The devil himself doesn't reveal his true form. He disguises himself as everything you've ever desired." Ophelia nodded in agreement. "Kael's right. There are countless false gods lurking in the shadows. That woman could be one of them." Cassius's gaze swept the room, his mind racing with doubts. He had always prided himself on his ability to discern truth from deception. But the Imperia's piercing gaze had left him unsettled. "Alright," Cassius said finally, his voice firm. "We'll proceed with caution. Our primary objective remains the same: to strengthen our cult. We need mortals to achieve that." Aria raised her hand, a hint of excitement in her voice. "I can help with that." Luna stepped forward, her eyes gleaming with enthusiasm. "I'll accompany

Aria." Ophelia nodded, a calculating glint in her eye. "Very well. You two will focus on recruiting mortals. The rest of us will devise a plan to…acquire Odessa." The cult members dispersed, their whispers and murmurs filling the air as they began to weave a web of deceit and manipulation. Cassius watched them, his mind still reeling from the Imperia's words: "You've succeeded in pissing off the false gods." A shiver ran down his spine. Had he underestimated the Imperia's power? Only time would tell.

Emberdale High's Cafeteria, Nicholas slid into a chair beside Calantha, Ayla, and Odessa, the hum of conversation and clinking silverware filling the air. Calantha's gaze locked onto Nick, a mischievous glint in her eye. "So, Nicky, do you love my sister?" she asked, her voice dripping with amusement. Nick's eyes widened, caught off guard. "Uh…what?" Ayla intervened, her voice soft but firm. "Nicky, you don't have to answer her." Calantha pouted, her eyes sparkling with teasing intent. "I think he does. Don't you want to know what dark and naughty fantasies Nicholas is keeping?" Nick's face flushed, and he stuttered, "I…love hanging out with her." Odessa chimed in, her tone playful but laced with sarcasm. "You hung out once, Nicky. And you shouldn't be calling that 'hanging out'." Ayla attempted to steer the conversation towards safer waters. "Can we talk about something else…please?" But Nick's words spilled out, unrestrained. "I love her, okay." Calantha's eyes lit up, and she purred, "Mm, mm, Nicky."

As they bantered, Odessa's gaze drifted towards the cafeteria entrance. A figure in a black hoodie caught her attention, their eyes fixed on their group. A shiver ran down her spine. "Guys, I'll be right back," Odessa said, pushing her chair back. She approached the mysterious figure, who turned and walked away. Odessa followed, her heart pounding in her chest. The figure stepped out of the school, into the crisp afternoon air. "Hey, hey," Odessa called out, her voice firm but cautious.

The figure stopped, and Odessa approached, her senses on high alert. "Why were you creeping on us?" The figure burst into a creepy, mirthless laughter.

"What? Did I say something funny?" Odessa asked. "I know what you and your little friends did weeks and weeks ago," the figure said and added, "And you saw that I saw what you did." Odessa's skin crawled. "I don't know what you're talking about." The figure produced three photos from their pocket, each depicting one of the mortals Odessa and her sisters had snatched for Cassius. Odessa's eyes widened, recognition mixed with alarm.

"Bet you just felt nostalgic, didn't you?" the figure said, their voice dripping with malice. "Because I just did." Odessa's face remained still, but her mind raced. "I don't know what you're talking about. And who are you?" The figure's laughter sent shivers down her spine. "Well, that's a one million dollar question, 'who am I?'"

Before Odessa could respond, the figure vanished into thin air. She spun around, but there was no one in sight. Ayla, Calantha, and Nick approached, concern etched on their faces. "Are you okay? You look like you've seen a ghost," Ayla asked. Odessa hesitated, unsure how to reveal the unsettling encounter. "I...," she began, but her words faltered. Calantha's eyes narrowed. "What?"

Odessa scanned their surroundings, ensuring they were alone. "Nothing, I'm fine." But the encounter left her with a haunting sense of unease, and the feeling that she was being watched.

Meanwhile in the Selenea Realm, The Imperia settled into her throne, her piercing gaze fixed on Maverick, who stood before her amidst the realm's breathtaking beauty. "Mother, don't you think we should force Odessa to come home?" Maverick asked, her voice laced with concern. The Imperia's expression remained serene. "She'll call for me, seeking my help." Maverick's eyes narrowed. "And you won't help, right?" The Imperia's words trailed off, but Maverick cut her off, her tone tinged with pain. "But she and her friends captured and caged me… for days. If that isn't torture itself, I don't know what it is." The Imperia's gaze softened, surprise etched on her face. "I had no idea." Maverick's voice dripped with sarcasm. "You what? I thought gods were omniscient." The Imperia's expression turned introspective. "There's only one God, and He is… omniscient. I believe we were created to be queens, kings, and rulers of our own realms… kingdoms." Maverick's eyes sparkled with determination. "Well, since you now know Odessa's been up to no good, what will you do, Mother?" The Imperia's voice was measured. "Everything has consequences and repercussions, I shall consider hers." Maverick's words spilled out, laced with skepticism. "She's your favorite, Mother. We know you won't do anything." The Imperia's gaze snapped back to Maverick, a hint of warning in her voice. "Are you questioning my authority?" Maverick bowed her head, her voice barely above a whisper. "No, Mother." With a subtle nod, Maverick departed, leaving the Imperia to her thoughts. The Imperia rose, her gaze drifting to the window, where her children gathered, their laughter and whispers carrying on the wind.

7

CHAPTER VII — Friday Night at Lake Luminaria.

Friday Night at Lake Luminaria, the warehouse loomed before them, its entrance a hive of activity. Calantha, Ayla, and Odessa, dressed to impress, stood at the door, unsure if they'd gain entry. The bouncer, Jamie, eyed them warily. "Sorry, ladies. You're not on the list," Jamie said. Just as they were about to leave, Nicholas appeared, a charming smile on his face. "Oh, wait. I invited them. They're with me." Jamie raised an eyebrow. "You did? Three of them?" Nick nodded. "Yes, I did. Can you let them in, please?"

With a nod, Jamie stepped aside, allowing the trio to enter. Inside, the music pulsed, and the crowd was abuzz. Nick took Ayla's hand, leading her away, leaving Calantha and Odessa to explore.

At the bar, they perused the offerings. "What can I get you ladies?" the bartender asked. Calantha raised an eyebrow. "A bar? In a freaking warehouse near a lake?" The bartender chuckled. "I know, right?" Odessa intervened. "Can you get us one of your finest drinks?" The bartender listed their options:

"Bloody Mary, Tequila shot, Kamikaze shot, or Apple Martini." Odessa opted for the Bloody Mary. "Uh… I think Bloody Mary will do, thank you."

The bartender prepared their drinks. "Here's your finest drink, ladies. And we have the finest guys too. Perhaps I could arrange that too." Calantha and Odessa exchanged a look, politely declining. "I'm Owen, by the way," the bartender added.

Meanwhile, Nick and Ayla sat in a corner, chatting. Nick's words slurred slightly. "I didn't know you were coming. I could've invited you." Ayla smiled. "We figured there'd be a party. So we came."

Nick leaned in, attempting a kiss. Ayla dodged, hinting she wasn't interested. "What's wrong?" Nick asked. Ayla hesitated. "Nothing… it's just…" Just then, Chloe appeared, her eyes flashing with anger. "Nick! You're dating her now?" Nick's response was laced with drunken bravado. "We're over, Chloe. Move on." Chloe's retort was venomous. "It's over when I say it's over. And couldn't you have chosen someone… more appealing?" Ayla stood, her eyes blazing. "What did you just say?" Chloe sneered. "You heard me." Ayla's slap echoed through the warehouse. Nick intervened, stopping the fight.

Calantha and Odessa watched from afar. Ayla glanced at the party goers nearby her sisters and her attention was drawn to two familiar faces - Aria and Luna, Cassius's cult members. Ayla pushed Chloe to the side to pass and approached her sisters.

"Recognize them?" Ayla asked, her voice low. Calantha and Odessa nodded in unison. "They're from Cassius's cult." Aria and Luna collected two mortals, heading outside. The sisters followed, determined to thwart their plans. Outside, the air was tense. Odessa confronted Aria and Luna. "Doing Cassius's dirty work, I see." Aria sneered. "Like Cassius said, we're doing what your false gods couldn't dare to do." Calantha chuckled. "Your encounter with the Imperia didn't scare you, I believe." Luna retorted. "She's no god, nor false god, but a witch." Ayla intervened. "What do you get for serving Cassius? Those powers won't go to you, but to him." Odessa's eyes narrowed. "You're not leaving with those mortals." Aria taunted. "What are you gonna do?" — "What am I gonna do? Well, why don't you take a swift guess?" Odessa asked but before Aria could take that guess. Odessa's hand striked Aria's chest. Aria flew backward, landing near the water. Luna let go of the mortals, frozen in fear. Calantha cast a spell, immobilizing the mortals, who were trying to run. Odessa approached Luna. "Want to take a guess, too?" Luna trembled, and Odessa sent her flying, joining Aria by the water.

The three sisters approached them. Odessa stood tall, her eyes locked onto Aria and Luna, her voice low and menacing. "Tell Cassius: no more mortals. Or he shall meet my darker side. And I don't think anyone has ever seen that side of me, and he wouldn't want to be the first." She paused, her gaze intensifying. "First tries are always dangerous." With that, Odessa's words hung in the air, a warning that sent a shiver down Aria and Luna's spines. "Go now, go on." Ayla said. Aria and Luna fled. "Let's get out of here," Odessa said, as the sisters walked away from the warehouse. "Yeah, let's," Calantha agreed. Ayla nodded. "Time to head home."

As they vanished into the night, the warehouse lights faded, leaving only shadows and secrets behind.

Meanwhile at the Order of the Eternal Flames, Aria and Luna burst into the dimly lit chamber, their bodies battered and bruised, blood dripping from their mouths. Cassius's eyes narrowed, concern etched on his face. "What happened to you?" he demanded. Aria winced, clutching her chest. "They stopped us from… taking mortals." Cassius's expression darkened. "Who dared to intervene?" Luna's voice trembled. "Odessa and her friends." Cassius's gaze intensified. "Odessa and her friends, you say? And what message did they convey?" Aria's words spilled out, laced with pain. "They said… no more taking mortals." Cassius's eyes flashed with anger. "Since when do they care about humanity?" Kael, ever the pragmatist, spoke up. "Perhaps we should lay low on taking mortals and revert to our old ways – sacrifice animals."

Cassius's response was swift and decisive. "No one is going back to those old ways." He turned to Aria and Luna, his voice dripping with venom. "We shall make them pay for what they did to you." — "They're powerful and we won't… " Aria attempted to protest, but Cassius cut her off. "We won't what? You tend to forget who we worship. I doubt the dark lord, prince of darkness, would let us fail in accomplishing one of his desires – to bring hell on earth." Ophelia's voice chimed in, eager to please. "What do you suggest we do, Cassius?" Cassius's smile was sinister. "Call on the dark lord, of course."

8

CHAPTER VIII — The Devil's Bargain: Trapped in Carnage.

The next morning, Odessa, Ayla, and Calantha gathered in their apartment, their conversation laced with anticipation and concern. "I believe Cassius will retaliate soon," Odessa said, her eyes locked on her friends. Ayla smirked, her voice dripping with sarcasm. "We'll be armed and dangerous, ready to take him down."

Meanwhile, in the depths of Cassius's cult, a sinister ritual unfolded. Cassius stood in his secretive prayer room, his voice echoing off the cold, dark walls. "Lucifer, prince of darkness, descend to me. Come, Lord, and appear before me, in all your majesty and power. Through your strength and dominion, reveal yourself, and grant me an audience. Hear my voice, and fulfill my deepest desire. Let your presence ignite the shadows, and let your will be done. I summon you, mighty Lucifer, come and claim your rightful place here on this mortal realm." The air in the room began to chill, a faint breeze whispering an ominous presence. A figure with horns materialized, shrouded in an ethereal glow that obscured its features. "Mortal, faithful servant, your devotion has summoned me," the dark lord declared, its voice like thunder in the shadows. "I sense your ambition, your hunger for power, and your willingness to surrender to the shadows. Speak your desire, and I shall grant it… at a price." Cassius's eyes gleamed with fervor. "I desire the power to bring hell on earth, to accomplish one of your desires. Grant me immortality and the strength to defeat anyone who dares to stop me." The room's temperature plummeted, the shadows seeming to twist and writhe like living serpents. The dark lord's response sent shivers down Cassius's spine. "Rise, Mortal, and unleash hell's fury." As suddenly as it appeared, the dark lord vanished, leaving Cassius bathed in an eerie silence. He approached a mirror dripping with blood, a creepy smile spreading across his face. "Time for a reckoning," he whispered, his eyes blazing with an otherworldly intensity.

As Nicholas strolled through the bustling streets with his friend Mike, a striking woman approached them. Her piercing gaze and enigmatic smile commanded attention. "Hey, boys," she said, her voice husky and confident. Nicholas and Mike exchanged skeptical glances, but remained silent. "I'm Ophelia," she continued, her eyes locked on them. "And I hold an invitation to a church where freedom awaits." Mike's curiosity got the better of him. "Are there beautiful women like you there?" he asked, flashing a charming smile. Ophelia's lips curled into a sly grin. "You'll have to find out for yourself, but I promise you, there won't be any disappointments." Mike turned to Nicholas, his eyes sparkling with excitement. "What do you say, buddy? A night at the church?" Nicholas hesitated, unsure. "I don't know, buddy." Ophelia's gaze narrowed, her interest piqued. "You're Nicholas Grey, aren't you?"

Nicholas's eyes widened, surprised. "How did you know my name?" Ophelia's smile grew, her voice dripping with intrigue. "Aren't you the famous Nicholas who's dating the three... weird sisters?" Nicholas's face flushed, defensive. "They're not weird. And I'm not dating them, just one of them. She's beautiful, and I think she might be the one for me." Ophelia's eyes glinted with amusement. "You're a bit of an oversharer, aren't you?" She paused, her expression turning mysterious. "How about you come to this location on this poster, and I'll tell you everything you want to know about these sisters... and the secrets they're keeping from you, despite calling you their friend?" Nicholas's curiosity was piqued. He took the poster, his mind racing with questions. "Okay, I'll be there."

As evening descended, Nicholas and Mike stood before the mysterious location, hesitation etched on their faces. "Should we go inside?" Nick asked, uncertainty creeping into his voice.

Mike's enthusiasm remained unwavering. "We're already here; might as well see it through. Now or never, buddy." With a deep breath, they stepped into the unknown. The building's interior was shrouded in darkness, except for a single spotlight illuminating a chair at the center. "This doesn't feel right," Nick whispered, unease growing. Mike attempted to reassure him. "Relax, buddy. Maybe the church is at the back, or they haven't set up the chairs yet." A sultry female voice echoed through the room, sending shivers down their spines. "Hey, boys." Mike's voice trembled slightly. "Ophelia, is that you? You've got the ladies with you?" Ophelia's response dripped with seduction. "My word is my bond. I told you there wouldn't be any disappointments." As they edged closer to the chair, a stunning woman emerged from the shadows, her movements fluid and menacing. She locked the entrance door behind them, trapping them. Ophelia flicked a switch, and the room erupted into light. Masks adorned the faces of numerous women lining the walls, their eyes glinting with an unsettling intensity. Ophelia approached Nick and Mike, her smile twisted. "Let me reveal the true reason you're here." Mike's voice trembled. "Please…" Ophelia's words dropped like a guillotine. "You're here so I can kill Nick." Nick and Mike's laughter was short-lived, suffocated by the ominous sound of knives being unsheathed. "I'm quite serious," Ophelia emphasized, her eyes glinting with malevolence. "Nick's dying today." Mike's terror was palpable. "Why am I here, then?" Ophelia's laughter sent chills down their spines. "You're a ladies' man, Mike. I used you to lure Nick here. You'll get none of the ladies' affection." Nick's pleas were laced with desperation. "You'll go to jail for this." Ophelia's response was a cacophony of laughter. "Oh, Nicky, you're about to witness real evil, and you think I'll get arrested? How quaint." A figure emerged from the shadows, sword in hand. With a swift, deadly motion, she pierced Nick's heart. He coughed up blood as Mike screamed in horror. "Poor Nicky, unable to utter your last words," Ophelia mocked, her laughter echoing through the room. Another woman struck, plunging a knife into Mike's chest. The two friends crumpled to the ground, their lives extinguished. Ophelia claimed their phones, capturing images of their lifeless bodies. With a twisted grin, she sent the photos to Ayla, a haunting message accompanying the gruesome visuals and a location where they're.

9

CHAPTER IX — Tears of Blood.

The following day, Ayla's world shattered as she gazed upon the gruesome images on her phone. Tears streamed down her face like rain, her heart heavy with grief. Her sisters, Calantha and Odessa, sensed her distress and rushed to her side. "Ayla, what's wrong?" Calantha asked, concern etched on her face. Ayla's voice trembled as she handed Calantha the phone. "Look…" Calantha's eyes widened in horror as she took in the graphic visuals. "Is that…Nicky?" she whispered, her voice cracking. Odessa gently took the phone from Calantha's shaking hands, her expression grim. "We need to find out who did this," she said, her eyes scanning the images for any clues. "There's a location attached to the message. Let's go." Ayla's legs felt like lead, but her sisters' determination propelled her forward. They arrived at the location, a nondescript building that seemed to mock them with its ordinariness. The air inside was thick with the stench of death.

Ayla's knees buckled as she saw Nicholas's lifeless body, his eyes frozen in a permanent stare. She crumpled to the ground, her tears falling onto his cold skin. "Nicky…no…please," she whispered, her voice shattered. Odessa's hand rested on Ayla's shoulder, a gentle comfort. "I'm so sorry, Ayla. Nick's dead." Ayla's gaze pleaded with Calantha, her eyes red-rimmed. "Can't you…can't you do something? Some magic to bring him back?" Calantha's face contorted in anguish. "Ayla, I'm sorry. Nick's gone forever. We can't bring him back." Ayla's body shook with sobs, her sisters' words piercing her like a dagger. She clutched Nicholas's hand, her fingers intertwined with his limp ones. "Why?" she wailed, her voice echoing off the cold walls. "Why did this happen?" Calantha and Odessa stood by, helpless to ease their sister's pain. They wrapped their arms around Ayla, holding her as she shattered into a million pieces. In that moment, time stood still. The world narrowed to a single, devastating truth: Nicholas was gone but was Ayla's heart forever broken?

Ayla clung to hope, her heart refusing to accept the brutal reality. She convinced her sisters to take Nick's lifeless body with them, leaving Mike's behind. The police soon arrived, and the gruesome discovery was broadcast on the news.

Two days passed, and Cassius's informant within the police department contacted him. "Have you seen the news?" the informant asked, his voice laced with caution. Cassius leaned back in his chair, his eyes narrowing. "I have better things to do, a world to conquer." The informant hesitated before speaking. "There's been a gruesome murder, and the way this person was killed…it bears your signature." Cassius's expression turned cold. "You think I had a hand in that?" The informant chose his words carefully. "All I'm saying is that you should question your people." The call ended, and Cassius's gaze lingered on the phone. He rose from his chair, his movements fluid and menacing. He strode to the cult's gathering place, where his followers sat in silence.

"Well, well, well," Cassius said, his voice dripping with sarcasm. "Someone has been really busy. I hear there's been a murder, and the police thinks we're involved." The cult members exchanged nervous glances, their denials tumbling out in unison. Just then, Ophelia slipped into the room, her eyes locked on Cassius. "I did the killing," she said, her voice steady. Cassius's smile grew, his eyes gleaming with approval. "This is good," he said, his voice dripping with excitement and added, "With the powers I hold now. We shall unleash hell's fury." Ophelia's curiosity was piqued. "What powers?" she asked, her eyes narrowing. Cassius's grin widened. "I had an audience with Lucifer Morningstar himself. He granted me immortality and the power to bring hell on earth, uninterrupted." Kael's eyes widened. "Lucifer spoke to you?" Cassius's voice dripped with reverence. "Not just spoke, but he granted me the power to fulfill our desires, together." The room fell silent, the cult members exchanging uneasy glances. Ophelia's gaze lingered on Cassius, her expression unreadable.

Ayla, meanwhile, held Nick's lifeless body, her heart heavy with grief. She whispered a promise to him, her voice barely audible. "We'll make them pay, Nicky. We'll make them pay."

10

CHAPTER X — The Spell of Revival.

Three weeks had passed since their encounter with Cassius's cult.

Odessa, Ayla, and Calantha sat atop rocks at Ember Peaks, strategizing against their foes. "How do we take down Cassius and his followers?" Calantha asked, her eyes fixed on the horizon.

"I think we start by eliminating his minions," Ayla suggested, her voice laced with determination. "But are we certain it's Cassius's doing?" Odessa questioned, her brow furrowed. "Evil permeates Emberdale." — "Of course, it's him," Ayla countered. "That's his MO – retaliation." Odessa nodded. "Then let's bring him down." As they spoke, the sky boomed, and a gentle breeze swept across the mountainside. Calantha's eyes sparkled. "I have an idea." — "Share it," Odessa encouraged. "What if we resurrect Nicky?" Calantha proposed, her voice barely above a whisper. Ayla's eyes widened. "You said that was impossible." Calantha nodded. "I've been researching witchcraft, and I found a resurrection spell. It's a long shot, but worth trying." Odessa's expression turned thoughtful. "If we succeed, Nicky will discover our secrets." Ayla's jaw set. "I'm willing to take that risk."

Meanwhile, at the cult's hideout… Cassius leaned back in his chair, a sly smile spreading across his face. "Ophelia, your manipulation skills are impressive. How did you persuade that mortal?" Ophelia shrugged. "Easy. Mortals are weak. Promise them something, and they'll follow." Cassius chuckled. "This realm will soon be ours." Ophelia's eyes narrowed. "With your immortality, you'll live forever, but we won't. I want immortality, Cassius." Cassius stood, his gaze drifting toward the window, "I'll discuss it with Lucifer."

Back at the hunters' apartment… Ayla, Calantha, and Odessa surrounded Nicky's body, lit candles casting a warm glow. Calantha invoked the Triple Goddess, calling for a full moon.
"Moon above, shine down on us,
Grant us the power, to revive and restore.
Full moon's light, we call to thee,
Illuminate our path, and set our hearts free.
By thy silvery glow, we seek to mend,
The bond between life and death, and make amends.
Hear our plea, dear Goddess of the night,
And fill our souls with thy radiant light."
As they chanted, the full moon rose, bathing the rooftop in its ethereal light. The trio smiled, and began the resurrection spell.

"From the shadows of death, we summon thee,
Back to the world of the living, where love awaits thee.
By the magic of the moon, we bind this spell,

Restore thy life force, and all shall be well.
Through the veil of the unknown, we call thy name,
Nicky, dear one, return to us, and reclaim thy flame.
From the realms of the afterlife, we guide thee back,
To the warmth of our love, and the light of the moon's track.
With every breath, we infuse thee with life,
And with every heartbeat, we restore thy vital strife.
Thy spirit, once lost, now finds its way,
Back to thy body, where love and light hold sway.
So let it be, with the power of the moon's pale glow,
We revive thy essence, and make thy heart whole."

As they finished the spell, Nicky's body stirred, confusion etched on his face. He was alive.

Nicky's eyes fluttered open, confusion etched on his face. "What's going on? And where am I?" he asked, his voice laced with disorientation. Ayla's hand wrapped around his, her touch warm and reassuring. "You're at our apartment, Nicky," she said softly.

Nicky's gaze drifted to his chest, where the memory of the fatal wound still lingered. He touched the spot, his eyes widening. "I saw myself die... What am I, back? What did you do?" Odessa's lips curved into a gentle smile. "Well, we kind of brought you back to the land of the living." Nicky's eyes snapped to Odessa, incredulity written across his face. "Brought me back? How? Are you an angel?" Odessa chuckled, her laughter warm and melodious. "Of course not, Nicky." Calantha's expression turned serious. "Let us tell you the truth, Nicky. I'm a witch, an Emberdale witch. Ayla is a creature from the Khaosia realm, and Odessa is from the Selenea realm. We're all immortal, meaning we can't die."

Nicky's eyes widened, his mind reeling. "I know what immortality means, but surely you're joking." Ayla stood, her movements fluid and deliberate. She grasped a knife and slid it across her throat. Nicky's eyes went wide as she dropped to the ground, her body still. "Are you all crazy? What kind of sick bullshit is this?" Nicky exclaimed, horror etched on his face. Odessa's voice remained calm. "Nicky, wait and see." Ayla rose from the dead, her movements eerily silent. Nicky stumbled backward, his eyes fixed on her. "What? How?" he stammered. Odessa's expression turned solemn. "I think we've shown you all the proof you need. Now, do you know who killed you?" Nicky's gaze faltered, memories resurfacing. "Some girl... She said her name was Ophelia. She invited Mike and me to a church, promising freedom." Ayla's eyes narrowed. "What girl? Can you describe her?" Nicky's brow furrowed. "Ophelia... She was beautiful, with piercing eyes. She said freedom awaited us at the church." Calantha's expression turned thoughtful. "What else do you remember?" Nicky's eyes clouded. "Where's Mike?" Odessa's voice softened. "Mike's dead, Nicky. And before you even think about it, no, we can't bring him back." Nicky's face crumpled, and he stood, his movements stiff. Without a word, he turned and left, leaving the trio in silence.

11

CHAPTER XI — Spellbound.

Emberdale High School, Nicholas, still reeling from Mike's passing, spent his lunch break with Austin. Calantha, Ayla and Odessa approached them, their presence a stark contrast to the mundane high school atmosphere.

"Nicky, can I talk to you?" Ayla asked, her voice laced with a mix of warmth and concern. Nicholas hesitated before nodding. "Oh... okay." As they stepped aside, Ayla's expression softened. "I'm glad you're back, Nicky." Nicholas's gaze drifted, his eyes clouding. "I was supposed to be dead. Now I have to feel the pain of Mike's death." Ayla's hand instinctively reached out, offering comfort. "You have me, I got you, Nicky." Nicholas's gaze snapped back to Ayla, his eyes narrowing. "Those two girls, are they friends with you?" He nodded toward Calantha and Odessa.

Ayla's expression faltered, her voice measured. "Friends with me? No, they're my sisters... and you know that." Nicholas's brow furrowed. "I don't know that, woman." Ayla's eyes searched his face, seeking a glimmer of recognition. "But you know me, don't you?" Nicholas's response cut deep. "I...

don't... know you, woman." Ayla's face fell, her eyes stinging. Nicholas turned, returning to Austin, leaving her standing alone. Calantha and Odessa approached, concern etched on their faces. Ayla's anger boiled over, her hand pushing Calantha. "You witch, what have you done?" Ayla demanded, her voice low and venomous. Calantha's eyes widened. "What are you talking about, Ayla?" Odessa intervened, her voice a soothing balm. "Come down, sisters. People are watching." Their voices dropped to a whisper. "Nick doesn't know who I am," Ayla spat, her words laced with pain. Calantha's expression mirrored shock. "What? That's impossible."

Ayla's accusation cut deep. "You wiped Nicky's memory?" Calantha's hands rose in defense. "I did not do such." Ayla's eyes blazed. "Well, then maybe your resurrection spell didn't quite fully work... or maybe you're just a weak witch." Odessa's calm demeanor attempted to mediate. "Surely, there's an explanation for all this. Let's not fight but work together to find out what went wrong." Ayla's response was icy. "I don't think I'll ever work with this witch again." Calantha's eyes pleaded for understanding. "Sister, you have to believe me. I didn't do anything to poor Nicholas." Ayla's pain simmered, her words laced with venom. "Then how do you explain this? He remembers you and Odessa but not me." Calantha's expression turned thoughtful. "I don't know how that's possible." Ayla's anger boiled over. "I believe you two orchestrated this because you weren't really fond of my relation with Nicky." Odessa's voice remained calm. "Sister, stop it."

Calantha's defense grew more adamant. "Maybe it would've been better if we didn't resurrect Nick. I felt your pain, the loss you felt, and helped you... and you accused me of messing with Nick's memory?" Ayla's response was a cold, hard truth.

"How could you?" Calantha's words poured oil on the flames. "Maybe it's a mortal disease… memory loss?" Ayla's eyes flashed. "No. You did something to him." Calantha's voice remained measured. "Nick's mortal… and every mortal is bound to suffer a horrible phase in their lives." Odessa's intervention was timely. "Calantha, stop pouring gasoline on the fire that's already burning." Ayla turned, her back to her sisters, and walked away, leaving Calantha and Odessa alone amidst the turmoil.

The next day, Maverick descended into the mortal realm, her presence a whispered rumor among the shadows. She sought out the one who had once captured her, Cassius. Their past encounter still lingered, a festering wound. Cassius's office was a sanctuary of power, its walls adorned with symbols of his dark ambitions. Maverick stood tall, her eyes locked on Cassius, who reclined in his chair, steepling his fingers. "I must admit, I'm intrigued," Cassius said, his voice laced with curiosity. "You willingly walked into the lion's den. What's your angle, Maverick?" Maverick's smile was enigmatic. "Maybe, or maybe not. I'm here to offer my assistance, to help you unleash hell's fury." Cassius's brow furrowed. "I'm still trying to understand our last encounter. The woman with the long white hair… what are you people?" Maverick's chuckle was low and husky. "We're creatures, out of this world. Immortal, some might say." Cassius's eyes narrowed. "False gods, I see." Maverick's amusement was evident. "You're still clinging to that theory?" Cassius leaned forward, his eyes piercing. "Why should I accept your offer?" Maverick's response was laced with venom. "Because I hate my sister, and I want her dead." Cassius's gaze turned calculating. "Odessa, isn't it?" Maverick's nod was curt. "Yes." A slow smile spread across Cassius's face. "It seems we share a common goal." Maverick's eyes sparkled with anticipation. "Well, then, what do you say?" Cassius rose from his chair, his movements deliberate. He extended a hand, and Maverick took it, their pact sealed with a firm handshake.

Their alliance was forged in darkness, a bond of mutual ambition and desire for destruction. The mortal realm trembled, unaware of the chaos that was to come.

The Rooftop Sanctuary, Calantha and Odessa sat together on the rooftop of their apartment, the city skyline stretching out before them like a canvas of twinkling lights. The air was heavy with the weight of yesterday's events, Ayla's absence a palpable reminder of the rift that had grown between them. "Sister, you didn't do anything to poor Nicholas, did you?" Odessa asked, her voice laced with concern. Calantha's eyes widened, her expression indignant. "Of course not, Odessa. I would never harm him."

Odessa's gaze searched Calantha's face, seeking reassurance. "Maybe Cassius has something to do with this too," Calantha ventured, her voice barely above a whisper. Odessa's expression turned thoughtful. "Calantha, look… I hate Cassius with all my guts, but we can't keep assuming that everything that happens to us is somehow his doing. Maybe the spell didn't work, and it's not your fault. It was your first time trying it." Calantha's shoulders sagged, her head nodding in agreement. "I suppose you're right, Odessa. I was so sure it would work…" Odessa's hand reached out, offering comfort. "Continue with your research, perhaps you might find something useful that we can work with." Calantha's determination reignited. "I will, Odessa. I won't rest until we find a way to restore Nicky's memories and bring Ayla back to us."

Together, the sisters sat in contemplative silence, the city lights twinkling like stars below, as they pondered their next move in the intricate dance of magic and mystery that had become their lives..

12

CHAPTER XII — Fires of Eternal Damnation.

The Darkest Hour, Emberdale, once a tranquil town, had succumbed to unrelenting darkness. The very fabric of its existence was now tainted by an evil so profound, it seemed irredeemable. Cassius, fueled by an insatiable thirst for power, had unleashed hell's fury upon the world. With Maverick's guidance, his cult had spread terror, ensnaring every soul in its path. For months, the devil himself seemed to walk among the people of Emberdale, as Cassius and Maverick's dominance went unchallenged. Their reign of terror appeared endless, a never-ending nightmare from which the town couldn't awaken.

But then, a glimmer of hope emerged. A brother, bound by blood to both Maverick and Odessa, descended into the mortal realm. His arrival marked a turning point in the battle between light and darkness. With his presence, the tide began to shift, and the apocalypse was halted. The brother's bravery ignited a beacon of hope in the hearts of Emberdale's residents. Though the town was forever changed, its people now knew that even in the darkest of times, salvation was possible. The question was, at what cost?

Atticus Moonridge stood tall, his piercing gaze sweeping across the assembly of the Order of the Eternal Flames. Cassius and Maverick, the masterminds behind the chaos, stood before him. Atticus's eyes locked onto his sister, his voice low and even.

"Sister, this is what you were created for?" Maverick's eyes narrowed, her voice laced with defiance. "What exactly was I created for, then, brother?" Atticus's response was firm. "To be in our realm, far away from this one." Maverick's laughter was cold, her words dripping with malice. "I don't have time for all this. This is my time, and no one shall stand in my way." Cassius, fueled by ambition, raised his hand, attempting to unleash his devil-given powers on Atticus. But Atticus was unfazed, his strength surpassing Cassius's. The dark magic faltered, and Cassius's eyes widened in surprise. Atticus's grip closed around Cassius's throat, his voice dripping with contempt. "What are you? Lucifer's pet?"

Cassius's words were strained, his voice barely audible. "I don't like repeating myself over and over again... But I will repeat this again for the last time. I'm doing what your false gods couldn't dare to do." Atticus's chuckle was low and menacing. "What? So, Lucifer's supposed to be the true God, or you supposed to be the true God?" Cassius's response was cut short as Atticus reversed back Cassius's powers back to the dark lord and Atticus's grip tightened, his neck snapping with a sickening crack. The lifeless body crumpled to the ground, and Atticus turned to Maverick, his eyes blazing with warning. "Well, Sister, are you going to stop this nonsense? Or shall I break yours too?" Maverick's voice trembled, her defiance wavering. "I'm your sister." Atticus's expression hardened.

"Not for long, conspiring against our own sister." Maverick chuckled and said, "She deserves everything that's coming her way." Atticus's words were laced with venom. "And what makes you the expert on what she deserves? Sister, stop this. Please don't force my hand." Maverick's plea was genuine, his voice tinged with sorrow. "Fine, brother," Maverick whispered, her submission palpable. As she spoke, the dark energy dissipating, hell's fury vanquished. Cassius's lifeless body lay at Atticus's feet, a testament to his unyielding resolve. The balance of power had shifted, and Atticus stood victorious, his sister's allegiance restored.

Deep within the Infernal realm, Lucifer Morningstar sat upon his throne, surveying the pandemonium before him. With a wave of his hand, he summoned Maze, his most trusted demon. "Fetch me the mortal, Cassius," Lucifer commanded, his voice like thunder. "I desire an audience with him." Maze vanished into the shadows, returning with Cassius in tow. The mortal's eyes widened as he took in the sights and sounds of the Inferno. Lucifer's gaze pierced Cassius like a dagger. "Well, Mortal, remember me?"

Cassius swallowed hard, his voice trembling. "Of course, I do… but why am I in hell?" Lucifer's smile was a cold, calculated thing. "You don't recall? You made a deal with me, the devil himself, Cassius. A deal that you failed to fulfill." Cassius's eyes darted wildly, memories flooding back. "Take me back to the land of the living, I shall fulfill your desires," he begged. Lucifer's laughter was like a crackling flame. "Oh, mortal, I gifted you with powers beyond your wildest dreams—immortality among them. Yet, they stripped those powers from you and broke your neck. How… pathetic." Cassius fell to his knees, pleading.

"Please, my lord." Lucifer's expression turned glacial. "You, Cassius, shall burn in hellfire for all eternity. Take him away, Maze."

With a cruel smile, Maze dragged Cassius screaming into the depths of the Infernal, his soul doomed to suffer the torments of hell.

13

CHAPTER XIII — Beyond Apocalypse.

Maverick and Atticus appeared at Odessa, Ayla, and Calantha's apartment, but Ayla was nowhere to be found. Odessa's eyes narrowed. "Brother, what brings you here?"

"I've come to stop the apocalypse," Atticus said, his expression stern. "And I succeeded." Odessa's gaze intensified. "Cassius unleashed hell on earth." Atticus's jaw clenched. "You no longer need to worry about him." Odessa's eyes widened. "What do you mean?" Maverick's voice was cold. "He's dead." Calantha's eyes sparkled with curiosity. "But rumors said he was immortal." Atticus's smile was faint. "I reversed his powers back to Lucifer."

Odessa's eyes locked onto Maverick. "And what about his minions?" Atticus shrugged. "They pose no threat now." Odessa's gaze returned to Maverick. "You helped Atticus?" Maverick's expression turned icy. "I was working with Cassius to bring you down, Odessa." Odessa's eyes flashed with anger, but she turned to Ayla, who had just entered the apartment. "Sister, are you okay? Where have you been?" Ayla's voice was barely audible. "Needed some time alone." Odessa's concern was palpable. "We were worried sick."

As they reunited, Atticus slipped outside, followed by Calantha. "Can I ask you something?" Calantha said, her voice low. "Sure," Atticus replied. "Is it possible to resurrect someone and when they're back from the dead they lose their memories?" Calantha asked, her eyes sparkling with curiosity. Atticus raised an eyebrow. "Are you into witchcraft?" Calantha's smile was mischievous. "I'm a witch." Atticus chuckled. "Memory loss during resurrection is unprecedented. Did you resurrect someone?"

Calantha nodded. "Part of their memory is gone." Atticus's expression turned thoughtful. "I think their memory will return eventually." Calantha's eyes lit up with gratitude. "Thank you."

Atticus's gaze turned playful. "How do you know my sister, Odessa?" Calantha's smile was sly. "We used to hunt mortals together." Atticus's eyes widened, surprised. "Right."

Back inside the apartment. "So, what now brother? Are you going home?" Odessa asked. "I think we'll stay on this realm a bit, right, Maverick?" Atticus said. "I suppose." Maverick said. "I want to learn more about humanity." Atticus said.

The next day, the Emberdale High cafeteria buzzed with students chatting and laughing. Calantha, Ayla, and Odessa navigated through the crowd, their eyes fixed on Nicholas, Chloe, Jasmine, and Austin, who sat together, an unlikely quartet. Ayla's voice cut through the din. "Hey, Nicky." Nicholas's gaze narrowed. "What do you want, woman?" Chloe jumped to his defense. "Yes, what do you want?" Odessa's smile was laced with sarcasm. "A simple 'Hey, Nicky' never hurt anyone. So, relax. You know what's funny? Nick's always treating you as an option, just a place, a soul in this case, that he runs to when he's afraid of facing his demons."

Chloe's eyes flashed with anger. "Nick and I love each other, okay? And it'll always be like that." Odessa's eyebrow arched. "Is that an assumption or a presumption?" Ayla turned to Jasmine. "You seem like a really good person. I don't understand how you put up with this loser." Nicholas's face reddened. "Okay, that's enough. Can you two take your stranger woman and leave, please." Calantha's smile was sweet. "With all pleasure, Micky." Nicholas corrected her, his tone sharp. "My name's Nick." Calantha's apology was laced with mockery. "Forgive me… Nick."

The sisters turned and walked to their own table, leaving the tense encounter behind.

As they settled in, Jamie Scratch, a familiar face from the Lake Luminaria warehouse party, approached their table. "Can I join you ladies?" Odessa's expression turned icy. "Wait, wait, wait. I remember you… from the warehouse party. Jamie… Jamie Scratch. Well, Mr. Scratch, I believe you turned us away, and I don't think you're welcome here unless someone comes to rescue you? Mm, mm. No one's coming, so beat it, Mr. Scratch." Jamie's face fell, and he retreated, his eyes cast downward. The sisters watched him go, their expressions unyielding.

At the fallen cult, Ophelia stood before the gathered members of the Order of the Eternal Flames, her voice filled with conviction. "We all witnessed Cassius's demise. Now, we need a new leader, and I believe I'm the right candidate. I was Cassius's loyal soldier."

Kael's eyes narrowed. "Will you ask the dark lord to bless us with powers, something Cassius refused to do?" Ophelia's determination was palpable. "That's my priority. We need powers to keep this church thriving."

Meanwhile, Maverick and Atticus strolled through the streets, their conversation relaxed. "Does Mother know you're here, brother?" Maverick asked. Atticus smiled. "She sent me. Does she know you're here?" Maverick hesitated, her voice barely above a whisper. "Uhm… uh… yes." Atticus chuckled. "Sister, we both know lying isn't your forte. Stop trying." Maverick's shoulders sagged. "Fine. She doesn't know. She wouldn't have let me come."

Atticus nodded knowingly. "Of course, she doesn't." Maverick's gaze turned introspective. "Brother, you once said we were created to rule our realm. Is that the only reason?" Atticus's expression softened. "That was just a calming words, sister."

Maverick's eyes sparkled with insight. "I now see why Odessa loves this mortal realm and wants to protect it. I think we were also created to help these mortals." Atticus raised an eyebrow. "That's preposterous, sister." Maverick's passion intensified. "Think about it. Why do we have this human form? We're creatures meant to inspire fear, but instead, we wear this mask to blend in with mortals." Atticus's attention was caught by an ice-cream shop. "Let's get some ice cream. You talk too much, sister."

Together, they entered the shop, Maverick's words lingering in Atticus's mind like a challenge.

14

CHAPTER XIV — The Dark Pact.

A month had passed since Cassius's demise. Calantha sat with Ayla in their cozy apartment, her expression veiled. Ayla's concern was palpable. "Calantha, are you okay?" Calantha's smile was forced. "What? Don't I look okay?" Ayla's eyes narrowed. "Sister, you don't look okay. Your skin is… aging… somehow. Are you still immortal?" Calantha's laughter was uneasy. "What do you mean? Of course, I'm immortal. I'm a witch, remember?" Ayla's gaze lingered on Calantha's hair, once a rich, dark mane, now dull and brittle. "And your hair looks different." Calantha's shrug was dismissive. "It's probably a phase and it'll pass."

Ayla's eyes sparkled with worry, but she stood, her voice gentle. "I need to go somewhere. See you later?" Calantha nodded, her smile faint. "Sure."

As Ayla departed, Calantha waited, her anxiety growing. She rose, her movements swift, and vanished into the heart of the woods. The trees loomed above, their branches twisted and ancient. Calantha's voice echoed through the clearing, her words a summons. "I know I wasn't supposed to summon you because I don't worship you, but I need a favor." The air shimmered, and the Dark Lord materialized, his angelic form tainted by goat's legs. His eyes gleamed with curiosity. "You're a witch, aren't you?" he asked, his voice low and husky. Calantha's nod was hesitant. "Yes." The Dark Lord's smile was enigmatic. "What do you desire?" Calantha's words spilled forth, her desperation palpable. "Well, it seems like my powers are kind of glitching. Disappearing, perhaps. The Triple Goddess I used to worship no longer replies to me." The Dark Lord's eyes sparkled with intrigue. "Well, I shall grant you some of my mystical powers… at a cost!" Calantha's plea was urgent. "Please!" The Dark Lord's laughter was menacing, his words laced with malice. "Every time you hear this sound, you'll know what to do." The air was filled with the haunting wail of crying babies. Calantha's eyes widened, horror dawning. The Dark Lord vanished, leaving her shaken. As the sound faded, Calantha realized the terrible price she must pay for her powers' return.

Calantha's footsteps echoed through the hospital's sterile corridors as she navigated the wards, her heart heavy with an unspeakable purpose. The sounds of new life and joyous tears drew her to a delivery room. She waited outside, her eyes fixed on the door, her resolve unwavering. As the doctors emerged, beaming with congratulatory smiles, Calantha's grip on her knife tightened. She slipped into the room, unnoticed, as the mother cradled her newborn, basking in the warmth of their first moments together. The tender scene before her only fueled Calantha's determination. Tears streamed down her face, a twisted mockery of the joy that filled the room. With a swift, merciless motion, she raised her knife and ended the baby's innocent life. Calantha vanished into the shadows, leaving behind a trail of horror and grief. The sound of crying babies still echoed in her mind, a haunting reminder of the Dark Lord's demand but then later the cries stopped.

Calantha returned to the apartment, her eyes sunken and her soul heavy. Odessa and Maverick exchanged concerned glances. "Are you okay, Calantha?" Odessa asked, her voice gentle. Calantha's smile was forced. "Uh… I'm okay." Maverick's gaze lingered on Calantha's shirt, her eyes narrowing. "Is that blood on your shirt?"

Calantha's laughter was uneasy. "Uhm… no… it's ketchup." Odessa's expression remained skeptical, but she said, "Ayla said she's at the food truck. Wanna go meet her?" Calantha's response was swift. "No, I'm fine. Just get me something on your way back."

Odessa nodded, her eyes still locked on Calantha's. "What about you, Maverick? Wanna go or should I also grab something for you?" Maverick's voice was low. "Grab something for me."

As Odessa departed, Maverick's gaze intensified, her hearing ability honed. "I know we're not friends, but there's something you're not telling Odessa." Calantha's denial was instinctive. "What? No." Maverick's tone was measured. "Did my sister ever tell you about the power of my hearing ability? One could say I'm close to being a God. When people pray, God hears their prayers. With me, it's different. When you talk, not pray, I hear you. I believe I heard you talking to the Dark Lord." Calantha's eyes darted, her composure cracking. "I… wasn't talking… to anyone." Maverick's smile was faint. "See? I was told that lying doesn't look good on me, I should stop trying. And now I'm passing those very same words to you: stop trying, it doesn't look good on you." Calantha's shoulders sagged, her secret spilling forth. "Yes, I talked to the Dark Lord. I was praying to the Triple Goddess, and they no longer reply to me, so I needed a new source of power. I couldn't be a powerless witch of Emberdale. Lucifer was my only option."

Maverick's expression turned somber. "But the price you're paying! Slaughtering of babies? Didn't he present several options?" Calantha's voice was barely audible. "No." Maverick's words cut deep. "You're no longer a good witch. But a witch that kills babies? That's a quite transition right there." Calantha's eyes pleaded. "Please don't tell Ayla and Odessa about this." Maverick's gaze lingered, her response measured. "You're suggesting that I should lie?" Calantha's desperation grew. "No, I'm suggesting that you don't tell them." Maverick's smile was faint. "Still considered lying." Calantha's voice cracked. "I'm pleading you." Maverick's nod was reluctant. "Fine. I won't tell anyone."

15

CHAPTER XV — The Warlocks' Quest.

The sunrise cast its golden glow over Emberdale as Calantha, Ayla, and Odessa made their way to school, clad in their crisp uniforms. Their path intersected with Nicholas, his eyes locking onto Ayla's. "Hey," Nicholas said, his voice tinged with a mix of curiosity and longing. Calantha and Odessa chimed in unison, "Hello, Nicholas." Ayla's silence was palpable, but Nicholas's gaze persisted. "Can I talk to you?" he asked, his tone low and urgent.

Ayla nodded, and they stepped aside, their conversation hushed. "I don't know what's going on, but I remember now... we were dating," Nicholas confessed, his eyes searching Ayla's. Ayla's expression softened, but her words were laced with conviction. "Oh, Nicky, were we?" Nicholas's response was resolute. "Yes."

Ayla's gaze dropped, her voice barely above a whisper. "Do you remember what happened when you were brought back to life. We told you we're immortal. I agree with my sisters now – dating a mortal is torture. You'll get sick, die, and leave me."

Nicholas's face twisted in determination. "I don't care about your immortality." Ayla's words spilled out, a mix of pain and resolve. "Well, I care that I'll get hurt in the end. So, Nicky, we're over. I think Chloe's good for you. Bye, Nicky."

Nicholas's protest was cut short as Ayla turned and rejoined her sisters. The trio headed to the toilets, their conversation hushed.

"Nick remembers me now," Ayla whispered to Calantha and Odessa. Calantha's smile was warm. "That's amazing." Ayla's voice was firm. "No. I believe you two were right. Dating a human isn't going to do me any good. So, Nicky and I are over."

Atticus strolled down the street, lost in thought, when he collided with a mysterious woman. Apologetic, he flashed a charming smile. "Hey, there. I'm Atticus." The woman's piercing green eyes sparkled as she replied, "Hey. I'm Jas... Jasmine."

Atticus's curiosity was piqued. "Haven't seen you around. I'm always walking down this street." Jasmine's raven-haired beauty seemed almost otherworldly. "Same. And you don't look like you're from here," she said, her voice husky.

As they conversed, four figures emerged from the shadows. Atticus sensed an eerie energy emanating from them – Silas Pierce, Seth Cohen, Luke Harrison, and Wystan Everett, four warlocks with an aura of darkness. "Hello, friends," Atticus said, his tone cautious. Luke, with piercing blue eyes, approached them. "I'm Luke. Do you know where I can find the Order of the Eternal Flames?" he asked, his voice low and mysterious.

Atticus shook his head. "I'm afraid I don't know where that is."

Luke's gaze flicked to Jasmine, a hint of recognition flashing across his face. "Hey," he said, before swiftly turning away, leaving Jasmine no chance to respond. The warlocks vanished into the night, leaving Atticus wondering about their intentions. Jasmine's eyes lingered on Luke's retreating figure, a whispered thought escaping her lips: "The Order... it can't be." Atticus's curiosity was piqued. "What's the Order of the Eternal Flames?" he asked Jasmine. Her eyes locked onto his, a hint of fear and mystery dancing within. "Something I thought was long forgotten because the leader of it died, Cassius." she whispered.

The night air grew thick with secrets, and Atticus sensed that his chance encounter with Jasmine and a warlock's query would unravel a dark, ancient mystery.

Atticus stepped into Odessa's cozy apartment, where the warm glow of candles and the aroma of brewing tea enveloped him. His friends, Maverick, Calantha, and Ayla, turned to greet him, their faces etched with concern. "There's something I need to tell you all," Atticus said, his voice low and serious. Maverick raised an eyebrow. "Spit it out, brother." — "I met four warlocks today. Possibly new to Emberdale." Calantha's eyes widened. "Warlocks" — "You heard me loud and clear," Atticus replied, his expression stern. Calantha's gaze burned with determination. "I must meet them and rebuild our witch kind." Atticus's expression turned grim. "They're up to no good." Calantha's brow furrowed. "What do you mean? You said you just met them." — "They're looking for something called the Order of the Eternal Flames." Ayla's eyes flashed with recognition. "That's Cassius's cult!" Atticus nodded. "Exactly! And you see why I'm saying they're up to no good?" Calantha's expression softened. "What if you're wrong?" Maverick intervened. "Trust him, he's never wrong." The room fell silent, the weight of Atticus's words settling upon them. The Order of the Eternal Flames, Cassius's notorious cult, was a whispered nightmare among witches. What did these warlocks want, and what darkness would they unleash?

CHAPTER XVI — The Order of the Eternal Flames.

Two days later, the four warlocks from Crescent Bay, Luke, Silas, Seth, and Wystan, finally tracked down the Order of the Eternal Flames. They infiltrated the hideout, expecting to confront Cassius, the cult's notorious leader. Instead, they found only four members: Kael, Ophelia, Aria, and Luna. "Finally, we found the cult," Luke announced, his eyes scanning the dimly lit room.

Ophelia stepped forward, her piercing gaze meeting Luke's. "Who are you supposed to be?" Seth chimed in, "Just four dudes looking for Cassius. We believe he's the one running this operation."

Kael snorted. "Haven't you heard the news? Cassius is dead. Died long ago." Luke raised an eyebrow. "Really? Then who's in charge?"

Ophelia's expression turned icy. "That would be me." Luke's gaze swept the room, sensing an unusual energy. "I don't know if you've noticed, but there's an overwhelming feminine aura here. I could've sworn I sensed it the minute I entered." Aria bristled. "You just came here to disrespect us?" Luke smiled, his eyes locked on Ophelia. "How did Cassius die?" Ophelia's voice dripped with venom. "Got his neck broken. How pathetic." Luke's eyes narrowed. "One could say you didn't like Cassius, or am I wrong?"

Ophelia's expression twisted. "Let's just say he was a piece of garbage." Kael chimed in, "Since Cassius isn't here, how about you leave?" Silas snickered. "Brother, come join us. One guy in a group full of women? Really sad. What are they telling you?" Luke shot Silas a warning glance before turning back to Ophelia. "Cassius's death doesn't change our purpose. We're warlocks from Crescent Bay, and we know you rely on Cassius's powers. We're here to offer our assistance… to inspire evil upon this realm." Ophelia's gaze lingered on Luke before responding, "Sounds tempting, but no." Luke's smile grew wider. "Come on, what will you do when they start coming for you? You can't inspire evil without powers."

Ophelia exchanged nods with her cult members. "Fine. But if we accept your offer, we must be exposed to the same energies as you." Luke's eyes sparkled with triumph. "I can arrange that."

Ophelia and Luke descended into Cassius's secretive sanctum, a place where darkness reigned supreme. The air was heavy with the stench of malevolence, and Luke's eyes gleamed with anticipation.

With a flick of his wrist, Luke summoned the Dark Lord. The room trembled, and an unearthly presence materialized before them. The Dark Lord's angelic form was a cruel jest, its beauty marred by the grotesque goat legs that seemed to defy the very fabric of reality. "My lord, it's Luke, your loyal servant," Luke declared, his voice dripping with devotion. The

Dark Lord's gaze narrowed. "Why am I being summoned?" Luke's smile was a thin, mirthless line. "I came to Emberdale to fulfill your desires, to inspire evil upon this realm. Mortals deserve everything that's coming their way." The Dark Lord's expression twisted into a grotesque grin. "Agreed. All flesh must die, and in horrible, painful deaths." Luke's eyes burned with an unholy fervor. "I need a favor first, my lord." The Dark Lord's gaze turned calculating. "Speak, but you know it comes at a cost." Luke's voice was laced with deference. "I desire that you bless this cult with powers, so they can aid me in our noble endeavor." The Dark Lord's gaze flicked to Ophelia, then back to Luke. "The very same cult of Cassius's?" Luke's expression turned reassuring. "Yes, but he's not here. You don't have to worry." The Dark Lord's laughter was a low, ominous rumble. "You tend to forget who you're talking to, Luke. I'm the Devil. I have Cassius in my realm, the Infernal. And I shall grant this cult with powers." With a wave of its hand, the Dark Lord vanished into thin air, leaving behind an eerie silence. The cult members erupted into jubilation, their faces aglow with an otherworldly energy. Luke's warlocks, however, exchanged knowing glances – they alone were immortal, while the cult members had been granted powers, but not eternal life.

Kael stepped out into the crisp evening air, searching for Wystan. He spotted the warlock lounging against the railing, his eyes fixed on some distant point beyond the horizon. "Mind if I join you?" Kael asked, approaching cautiously. Wystan's gaze flickered to Kael, his expression unreadable. "I don't." Kael sat beside him, his curiosity getting the better of him. "You mentioned you're warlocks. What's your coven?" Wystan's eyes seemed to cloud over, his voice taking on a hint of mystery.

"Mystical Muses."

Kael's eyes widened. "I've heard of you. You're… infamous." A faint smile played on Wystan's lips. "We have our reputation." Kael leaned in, his voice barely above a whisper. "What's it like, being a witch?" Wystan's smile vanished, replaced by a stern expression. "I'm not a witch, mortal. I'm a warlock." Kael's brow furrowed. "But I thought the Dark Lord granted immortality to his followers?" Wystan's eyes flashed with a warning, and he raised his hand, his fingers brushing against Kael's forehead. "Forget this moment, let it fade," he whispered. Kael's thoughts grew hazy, his memories slipping away like sand between fingers. He blinked, confusion etched on his face. "What am I doing here with you?" Wystan's expression turned neutral. "I believe you wanted to thank us for speaking to the Dark Lord on your behalf." Kael's eyes narrowed, trying to recall. "Oh… yeah. That's right." Wystan nodded, his gaze returning to the horizon. "You can leave now." Kael pushed to his feet, a lingering sense of unease. "Thanks, I guess." As he headed back inside, he couldn't shake the feeling that something had been erased, hidden from him. He glanced back at Wystan, but the warlock's face remained enigmatic, his secrets locked behind an impenetrable mask.

$$17$$

CHAPTER XVII — Twin Terrors.

Nicholas and Chloe lounged together in his room, the tension between them palpable. Chloe's voice was laced with a mix of sadness and resignation as she spoke. "I think they were right," she said, her eyes fixed on some point beyond Nicholas.

He frowned, confusion etched on his face. "What are you talking about?" Chloe's gaze met his, her expression a mask of vulnerability. "Those weird sisters. They said you only see me as your second option. And I think they're right." Nicholas shifted uncomfortably, his mind racing. "What are you talking about, Chloe? That's not true." Chloe's voice trembled. "I saw you talking to Ayla yesterday. From where I was, it looked like the conversation didn't go as smoothly as you'd hoped." Nicholas sighed, rubbing his temples. "Chloe, Ayla and I broke up. You're my only option now." Chloe forced a smile, but it faltered, revealing the pain beneath. "You see what I mean, Nick? You and Ayla broke up, and now you're running back to me because you know I love you. But, Nick, I…I deserve better than to be your consolation prize." Nicholas reached out, "Listen, Chloe, I'm sorry—" but Chloe's words cut him off. "It's fine, Nick," she interrupted, her voice firm. "I don't think we should hang out anymore." Nicholas's eyes widened as Chloe stood up, her movements swift and decisive. "Come on, Chloe, I made a mistake. I'm sorry," he pleaded, but she was already walking away. The door closed behind her, leaving Nicholas alone with his regret. He slumped back onto his bed, wondering how things had gone so wrong.

Odessa's apartment was dimly lit, the only sound the soft hum of the city outside. She sat with her sisters, Ayla and Calantha, their faces illuminated by the faint glow of candles. "What do you think these warlocks want?" Odessa asked, her voice low and cautious.

Calantha's expression turned grave. "It's obvious. They're here to finish what Cassius couldn't." Ayla nodded in agreement. "I think Calantha's right. Whatever they plan, it can't be good." Calantha's eyes sparkled with determination. "What if I talk to them? I'll tell them I'm a witch. Maybe they'll listen." Ayla's brow furrowed. "I don't think that's a great idea, Calantha. What if they don't believe you?" Odessa's gaze dropped, avoiding eye contact. "Besides, if they're with the Order of the Eternal Flames…they probably praise Lucifer. You don't exactly…align with their beliefs, do you?" Calantha's jaw set. "Perhaps you're right, but I should try. We can't just sit back and do nothing." The sisters' uneasy silence hung in the air, heavy with unspoken concerns and uncertain futures.

Evening that day, Calantha trailed Seth, one of the warlocks, through Emberdale's winding streets. Her footsteps silent, she followed him for ten minutes before he stopped and turned.

"Hey, are you following me?" Seth asked, his eyes narrowing.

Calantha feigned innocence. "What? No." Seth's gaze lingered, unconvinced. "You are." Calantha's demeanor shifted, her voice taking on a hint of mystery. "I happened to hear that four warlocks visited Emberdale." Seth's expression turned skeptical. "Woman, I don't know what you're talking about." Calantha's words dripped with conviction. "I'm a witch, Emberdale witch." Seth raised an eyebrow. "I'm supposed to believe what you're saying?" Calantha's smile hinted at secrets. "I could show you proof, if that's what you want." Seth's curiosity got the better of him. "Go ahead, show me."

Calantha's eyes sparkled in the fading light. "Not here. Mortals…we both know what they do to witches." Seth nodded, and they slipped into the woods, the trees casting long shadows.

Calantha stood before Seth, her hands weaving a gentle pattern. "By moonlit whispers, ancient might, I call forth crystal, shining bright. From realms of mystic, hidden deep, Bring forth the orb, in mystic sleep." A soft glow emanated from her hand, and a crystal orb materialized, pulsing with ethereal light. Seth's eyes widened. "Incredible." Calantha's smile hinted at triumph. "I like to believe that you now believe me when I say I'm a witch." Seth nodded, his expression thoughtful. "Yes, I believe you." Calantha's gaze met Seth's, a spark of understanding passing between them. As they sat on a fallen log, Seth asked, "You pray to the Dark Lord, right?"

Calantha's voice was laced with reverence. "Yes, the devil himself." Seth's eyes narrowed slightly. "I see. And what's your coven?" Calantha's expression turned somber. "It was the Church of Shadows. Destroyed by witch hunters…they discovered us, and the rest is history. Now, I pray to the Dark Lord alone." Seth's expression softened. "I'm sorry to hear that." Calantha's gaze drifted, haunted by memories. "I'm over it. What's your coven?"

Seth's voice was low, his words measured. "The Order of the Eternal Flames." Calantha's eyes sparkled with interest. "I think I might have heard about it." Seth's gaze locked onto hers. "Oh? Have you?" Calantha's smile hinted at secrets. "Yes." Their conversation hung, suspended in the darkness. Suddenly, Calantha's gaze snapped back to the present, her expression twisted by an inner turmoil, sound of crying babies. "Excuse me."

Seth called out, but Calantha vanished into the darkness, driven by a dark devotion.

Calantha's feet carried her through the streets, her heart pounding to the rhythm of the Dark Lord's call. She collided with a woman carrying twins, one on her back, one in front. "Do you need some help?" Calantha asked, her voice laced with false concern. The woman hesitated, "I…I think I'm okay, but thank you." But Calantha's grip on the front baby tightened. Her smile disarmed the woman. "I should help. It's not every day I meet someone as…fortunate as you." 5 minutes later, they arrived at the woman's house. Put down the babies.

The woman's unease grew, but Calantha's words dripped with sweetness. "This house is immaculate. I'm sure it has nothing to do with the fact that your kids are angels. Where's their father, the likely candidate for Father of the Year?" The woman's discomfort intensified. "Thank you…their father is…working, probably on his way back now." Calantha's gaze roamed the woman's home, her eyes drinking in every detail. "What can I give you as a token of appreciation?" the woman asked, her voice laced with unease. Calantha's smile twisted, revealing her true nature. "One of your babies." The woman's eyes widened in horror. "What?" Calantha's voice was low, menacing. "I said I'd like one of your babies as a token of appreciation." The woman attempted to scream out for help but her scream was silenced by Calantha's spell, her mouth disappearing. Calantha's eyes gleamed with malevolence as she immobilized the woman.

With a twisted grin, Calantha slaughtered the twins, their cries echoing in the woman's mind forever. Calantha vanished into the night, leaving behind a trail of horror. Seth, still in the woods

18

CHAPTER XVIII — Shadows of Deceit.

The afternoon sun cast its warm glow over the apartment, but Calantha's heart was chilled by the sudden presence of the Dark Lord. His dark, ethereal form materialized before her, his eyes burning with an otherworldly intensity. "My lord," Calantha whispered, her voice trembling with reverence.

"I have the most darkest devotion for you," the Dark Lord declared, his voice like a cold breeze. "Which will help you and help me."

Calantha's curiosity was piqued. "What is it, my lord?" But before the Dark Lord could respond, his gaze flickered towards the window. Calantha followed his gaze, but saw no one. The Dark Lord vanished into thin air, leaving her bewildered.

Unbeknownst to Calantha, Odessa had witnessed the entire encounter from outside the window. Her eyes widened in shock as she processed what she had seen. She quickly retreated, not wanting to be discovered.

Odessa hastened to the mountains, where Ayla sat serenely, basking in the beauty of the blue sky. "We need to talk," Odessa said, her urgency evident. Ayla turned to her sister, a hint of annoyance on her face. "Can it wait? Today's day is beautiful, and I just want to observe it in peace... please." Odessa's expression was grave. "It's about Calantha." Ayla's interest was piqued. "She's just going to ruin my day, even when she isn't here. Okay, what about her?" Odessa's words spilled out in a rush. "Have you noticed anything different about her? Maybe changes in certain things?"Ayla's brow furrowed. "No, why's that?" Odessa's voice dropped to a whisper. "I don't know. Something's different. I saw her talking to the Dark Lord, just before I came here." — "The dark lord?" Ayla asked. Odessa's gaze was intense. "I think she prays to the Dark Lord." Ayla's eyes widened in shock. "She what now?" — "Shocking!" Odessa said. Ayla's mind reeled. "Does she know that you know... we know?" Odessa shook her head. "No. I think we should let her tell us. Perhaps we can hint at it here and there until the truth is revealed." Ayla nodded, her expression thoughtful. "Okay. That could work."

The sisters sat in silence for a moment, observing the sky, their minds consumed by the secrets Calantha kept.

Luke settled into his seat, flanked by Silas and Ophelia. The air was thick with anticipation. "You mentioned something the other day," Ophelia began, her eyes locked onto Luke. "You asked me what I'd do when 'they' start coming for me. Who did you mean by 'they'?" Luke's gaze was piercing. "I think you know very well."

Ophelia's expression remained enigmatic. "Trust me, I wouldn't have asked if I knew. So, who?" — "The false gods," Luke replied, his voice low and ominous. Ophelia's eyes sparkled with intrigue. "Praise Satan. That's the same theory that got Cassius's neck broken." Luke's interest was piqued. "With that, I presume he encountered one of the false gods?" Ophelia's smile hinted at secrets. "Not sure if she was a false god, but we had an encounter with someone divine." Silas's brow furrowed. "She?" Ophelia's gaze narrowed. "Yes, she. Why do I get the feeling that you guys always think women aren't incapable of ruling? Firstly, you question me being the leader of this cult, and now you're asking me this?" Silas's expression turned conciliatory. "Forgive us, Ophelia. In my 147 years, I've never seen women rule men. So, I gotta question everything that seems…insane." Ophelia's eyes glinted with amusement. "Hundred and forty-seven, you say?"

Silas nodded, his expression sheepish. "Was I not audible enough?" Luke's laughter was husky. "Enough. I think it's time we send potent messages to these false gods. Killing someone divine would be just perfect." Ophelia's smile was sinister. "Well, I happen to know someone." Luke's gaze locked onto Ophelia. "Who?" — "Odessa Moonstone," Ophelia replied, her voice dripping with malice. Luke's eyes sparkled with anticipation. "Well, well, then. She shall meet her demise." The cult's hideout seemed to darken, as if the shadows themselves were closing in on Odessa.

The Infernal Realm, Lucifer Morningstar rose from his throne, his piercing gaze fixed on Beezlebul, the lord of flies. The air was heavy with the stench of brimstone and decay. "I require your presence in the mortal realm, Beezlebul," Lucifer commanded, his voice like thunder. "I am weary of being trapped here, awaiting the cult's progress. Remind them to inspire evil, to make mortals praise my name." Beezlebul bowed. "I shall deliver your message, my lord." With a flicker of darkness, Beezlebul vanished from the infernal realm, reappearing in the mortal world.

The Cult's Hideout, Luke, Ophelia, and Silas huddled in their dingy lair. Suddenly, a figure materialized before them, its presence making the air thick with malevolence. Beezlebul's eyes gleamed with an otherworldly intensity. Ophelia took a step back, her hand on the dagger at her waist. "Who are you?" she demanded. Silas's voice was laced with reverence. "This is Beezlebul, king of hell." Luke's gaze narrowed. "What brings you to our humble abode, Beezlebul?" Beezlebul's smile was a twisted, fly-like grimace. "The dark lord grows impatient. He demands your progress, your devotion. Fulfill his desires, or face his wrath." Ophelia's eyes flashed with determination. "We're working on it." Beezlebul's warning was unmistakable. "Don't make him wait. He doesn't tolerate delay." With a burst of noxious air, Beezlebul vanished, leaving the cultists to ponder his ominous message. Luke's eyes locked onto Ophelia. "We need Odessa, and fast." Ophelia's gaze was calculating. "How do you propose we kill her?" Luke's grin was cruel. "Use your powers, Ophelia. It's easy peasy, lemon-squeezy." Ophelia's expression turned icy. "You're sending me?" Luke's tone was laced with menace. "Unless you'd rather return your powers to the dark lord."

19

CHAPTER XIX — Magic and Mayhem.

The Next Day, Luke and his cult members convened in their dingy lair, surrounded by flickering candles and the stench of decay. Their evil plan was taking shape. "I propose we lure Odessa here, rather than risking a confrontation on her turf," Aria suggested, her eyes gleaming with malice. Silas raised an eyebrow. "How do you intend to accomplish that?" Aria's smile was sinister. "Odessa has a weakness for mortals. If we capture a few and hold them hostage, she'll come to us." Seth's interest was piqued. "Which mortals is she closest to?" Aria's gaze turned calculating. "Nicholas is her most vulnerable link. Chloe, Jasmine, and Austin are also within her circle." Luke's eyes sparkled with anticipation. "Let's procure Nicholas, then." A week passed, and Nicholas strolled through the deserted streets, lost in thought. Suddenly, he sensed being watched. Wystan, Seth, and Kael emerged from the shadows. "Hey, friend," Wystan said, his tone deceptively friendly.

Nicholas's instincts screamed warning, but he replied casually, "Wassup?" — "We're lost," Wystan continued. "Could you help us find a place of freedom?" Nicholas's unease grew. "Freedom? Why am I suddenly getting a sense of Déjà Vu?" Kael's eyes glinted. "Maybe you've been to this place before." Nicholas's instincts screamed danger. "I can't help you. I gotta go." Seth's grip on Nicholas's hand was like a vice. "Where do you think you're going?" Nicholas tried to shake off Seth's hold. "Please let go."

But Seth's eyes flashed with malevolence, and he cast a sleeping spell. Nicholas's world went dark, and he collapsed into Seth's waiting arms.

Two Weeks of Silence, the cafeteria buzzed with students, but Austin and Chloe's worried expressions stood out. They approached Ayla, Calantha, and Odessa, their usual banter replaced with concern. "What do you want?" Ayla asked, eyeing them warily. "You're dating Nick's friend now? How hoe of a mortal are you?" Calantha and Odessa burst into laughter, but Austin's serious tone cut off their amusement. "Nick's missing," Austin said, his voice laced with anxiety. Ayla's expression changed from indifference to shock. "What?" Odessa's eyes snapped to attention. "For how long?" — "It's been two weeks now," Austin replied, his face etched with worry. Ayla's expression turned icy. "And why should we care? We're no longer hanging out with poor Nicholas, and we don't care about him." Chloe's gaze held a hint of desperation. "I know deep down you still care about him, Ayla. Even if you tell yourself that you don't, you know that's not true." Calantha and Odessa exchanged a knowing glance. "Does the police know?" Odessa asked, her tone serious. Austin nodded. "Yeah, but they're not being helpful." Calantha's brow furrowed. "What makes you think we can help?" Chloe's eyes pleaded. "You're the closest ones to Nick. Please." Ayla's expression softened, despite her attempts to appear indifferent. "Okay, we'll help," Odessa said, her voice firm. "But we can't discuss it with you, mortals. Beat it." Austin and Chloe exchanged a confused glance. "What?" they said in unison. Odessa pressed, her tone brooking no argument. "I said beat it." With that, Chloe and Austin left, leaving the trio to ponder the ominous news.

"Now I have no doubt this has something to do with us," Odessa said, her eyes narrowing. Ayla's gaze turned intense. "You think Cassius's minions are doing what Cassius couldn't finish?" Odessa nodded. "They see us as a threat. We need to send them a message." Ayla's smile was menacing. "Or maybe we'll just show up at their cult." Calantha's eyes sparkled with determination. "Let's do it."

The Cult's Hideout, Nicholas slumped in the wooden chair, his wrists and ankles bound by thick ropes. Two weeks of dehydration and beatings had taken their toll, his face a mess of bruises and lacerations. Luke's voice dripped with malice as he taunted, "It's been two weeks, Nicholas. Where are your friends? Or are they too busy to care?" Nicholas remained silent, his eyes cast downward.

Ophelia chimed in, her voice laced with venom, "I think they got the message, Luke. They'll come for him soon enough." As if on cue, four figures materialized inside the cult's hideout. Odessa, Ayla, Calantha, and Atticus formed a united front, their eyes fixed on Nicholas. Seth's gaze locked onto Calantha, a flicker of surprise crossing his face. "Oh, hello! You're with them?" Calantha's expression remained serene. "I am. And Nicholas is coming with us." Luke sneered, his eyes glinting with malevolence. "No one is going anywhere with anyone."

Odessa stepped forward, her voice dripping with menace. "You want me? Why not come for me instead?" Luke's glance darted to Aria before responding, "We snatched one of your precious mortals, and you came running. Clever, don't you think?" Odessa's eyes flashed with anger. "What's clever is when I skin you alive!" Luke snickered. "I didn't believe it when I was told you'd literally go that far for a mortal." Odessa's smile was icy. "Believe it now." With a swift motion, she unleashed her powers, sending Luke and his followers flying across the room. Ophelia remained still, her eyes fixed on Odessa. "Powerful?" Odessa taunted. "Interesting." Ophelia's voice dripped with malevolence. "I pray to the dark lord, and you know what comes next." The air seemed to charged with anticipation as Ophelia summoned her powers, striking Odessa with a blast of dark energy. Calantha stepped forward, her eyes blazing with fury.

The two witches clashed in a spectacular display of magic, their powers locked in a fierce battle. Ayla rushed to Odessa's side, helping her to stand. Atticus, Ayla and Odessa faced Luke and his followers. The fight raged on, the cult's hideout echoing with the sound of crashing bodies and shattered furniture. By the end of it, everyone was battered and bruised, Luna lying motionless on the ground.

Odessa, Atticus, Ayla, Calantha, and Nicholas stumbled toward each other, their bond stronger than ever. "Lacunae magicae," Calantha whispered, her eyes shining with exhaustion. The group vanished into thin air, leaving the cult's hideout in shambles.

The group appeared back at their apartment. Calantha's slender fingers traced gentle patterns on Nicholas's battered skin. Her voice whispered a soothing melody, imbuing the air with healing magic. "By soothing powers, I call upon thee," she murmured, her eyes closed in concentration. "Healing energy, calm Nicholas's body. Ease the pain, reduce the swell, restore his skin, all wounds to compel." As she spoke, a warm, golden light began to emanate from her fingertips, enveloping Nicholas's bruised flesh. The air seemed to vibrate with calming energy, soothing his ravaged skin.

Calantha continued, her words weaving a spell of restoration. "With gentle touch, I mend thy flesh. Nicholas's bruises fade, new skin to mesh. May comfort and peace envelop thee, and healing magic…" She repeated the incantation twice more, her voice growing stronger with each iteration. The golden light intensified, illuminating the darkened room. As the final words left her lips, Nicholas's bruises vanished, replaced by smooth, unblemished skin. His eyes fluttered open, wonder etched on his face. "Calantha?" he whispered, his voice filled with awe. Calantha's smile was radiant. "You're fine, Nicky."

20

CHAPTER XX — Fractured Bonds.

Two days later, Emberdale High's cafeteria buzzed with lunchtime chatter. Ayla, Calantha, and Odessa huddled together, their conversation a stark contrast to the lighthearted atmosphere.

"That day was literally the worst," Odessa said, her voice laced with frustration. "Can I say something?" Ayla asked, her eyes sparkling with a hint of mischief. Calantha and Odessa nodded in unison, intrigued. "We managed to take down one of them," Ayla began, her voice low and determined. "Why not try to eliminate the rest? They'll only keep harassing us." Calantha's expression turned thoughtful. "That won't be easy. The four warlocks are immortal, and the rest are mortal." Odessa's eyes narrowed. "Do you think the dark lord granted them powers?" Ayla nodded. "Yes." Odessa's voice dripped with disdain. "Desperate, indeed, to make a deal with the devil." Their conversation was interrupted by the arrival of Nicholas, Chloe, Austin, and Jasmine. "Hey, guys," Chloe said, her smile faltering as she met the trio's stoic gazes. Odessa, Ayla, and Calantha offered only faint smiles in response. "Thanks for helping us," Chloe continued, her tone tentative. "What did you do?" Odessa's eyes sparkled with sarcasm. "Shouldn't Nicky be the one thanking us? We saved him, after all." Nick's face flushed as he stepped forward. "Thank you, Ayla, Calantha, and Odessa."

Ayla's smile was sweet but brief. "Pleasure, Nicky." The tension was palpable as Ayla turned her attention to Chloe. "So, what now? You and Nick picking up where you left off?" Chloe's eyes darted to Nick before responding. "Uh, no. Nick and I broke up. It was mutual." Jasmine raised an eyebrow. "Was it, really?" Chloe's voice was firm. "Yes, Jasmine. It was." Odessa's patience wore thin. "I think we're done here. Why don't you all…beat it?" Austin, however, lingered. "I like you, Odessa. Would love to take you out sometime." Odessa stood, her eyes locking onto Austin's. "Sorry, but I won't be messing around with mortals. You'll die soon, leaving me sad, broken, and lonely. Probably on drugs." Austin's face fell. "What? That's weird." Odessa's tone turned icy. "Let me be clear: no, I won't go out with you." With that, Austin, Chloe, Nicholas, and Jasmine beat a hasty retreat, leaving the trio to their thoughts.

Evening descended upon the apartment, casting a warm orange glow over Odessa, Ayla, Calantha, Maverick, and Atticus as they lounged together, lost in thought.

"Odessa, Maverick and I are returning home," Atticus announced, his voice tinged with a hint of longing. Odessa's gaze remained fixed on the ceiling. "Travel safe, brother and sister." Atticus's eyes locked onto Odessa's. "You should come with us." Odessa's expression turned resolute. "And leave my sisters here?" Maverick's voice chimed in, "We are your family, bound by blood, not words." Odessa's tone remained firm. "Regardless,

I'm not leaving. Say hi to everyone for me. It's been ages." Calantha's gentle voice intervened, "Odessa, it's fine. Ayla and I will be okay. You can go with them." Ayla's skepticism was palpable. "Will we?"

Odessa's response was immediate. "I'm not going anywhere." Atticus's words dripped with disappointment. "The love you show these mortals is not the same love you show us, your own family. You're choosing them over us." Odessa's eyes met Atticus's. "Brother, listen. I'll come back when I'm done with my task here."

Maverick's curiosity was piqued. "What task, Odessa?" Odessa's silence was telling. Maverick's voice turned cold. "What if these mortals you're trying to protect invade our realm? Will you help them destroy us? Of course, you will." Odessa's response was adamant. "That's preposterous. They won't, and if they do, I won't help them." Atticus's words hung in the air like a challenge. "Stay, then. Maverick and I are leaving." Odessa's voice trembled. "But the fight isn't over yet." Atticus's expression turned resolute. "That's not our fight, Odessa. It's yours. Deal with your own problems now." Odessa's eyes searched Atticus's. "Are you abandoning me, brother?" Atticus's response was laced with a hint of sadness. "I guess I'll see you...never again." With that, Maverick and Atticus joined hands, their bodies dissolving into thin air as they vanished into their realm, Selenea. The apartment fell silent, leaving Odessa, Ayla, and Calantha to ponder the weight of Atticus's words. Ayla's gentle voice broke the silence. "Are you sure you're making the right decision by staying here?" Odessa's resolve remained unwavering. "I'm sure."

21

CHAPTER XXI —Enchanted Lives, Entwined Fates.

The Cult's Hideout, Ophelia's eyes blazed with fury as she confronted Luke and his warlocks. "I just lost Luna," she spat, her voice trembling. "Wasn't she immortal? Are we even immortal?" Luke's expression turned cautious, but his words were laced with indifference. "You're mortal, Ophelia." Ophelia's anger boiled over. "You didn't tell me these powers didn't come with immortality. I wouldn't have risked my life fighting that witch if I'd known." Luke shrugged, his nonchalance fueling Ophelia's ire. "I'm glad I didn't tell you." — "That's not the point!" Ophelia's voice rose. "I could have died. These powers are useless without immortality. How do you expect me to fight a witch who's immortal? She's never going to die." Luke's smile was condescending. "But she can feel pain, can't she?" Ophelia's eyes narrowed. "I want immortality." Luke's tone turned patronizing. "You should be grateful the dark lord granted you powers. You would have died already without his involvement." Ophelia's determination hardened. "I'll summon him myself." Luke's laughter was laced with scorn.

"What makes you think you have the ability to summon him whenever you want?" Ophelia's confidence didn't waver. "I have powers." Luke's amusement turned to anger. "Regardless of your powers, you can't summon him. It's impossible." Kael's arrival interrupted the tense standoff. Ophelia turned to him, her words spilling out in a rush. "Did you know we could have died that day of the fight?" Kael's laughter caught her off guard. "Died? We can never die, we're immortal, remember?" Ophelia and Luke exchanged a weighted glance. Kael's confusion was palpable as he turned to Luke. "We're immortal, aren't we?" Luke's response was laced with regret. "I'm afraid not." Kael's anger simmered, but Luke's powers restrained him. "No, no. Maybe you're mortal because you were born that way." Kael's eyes narrowed. "But Cassius was born mortal, and the Dark Lord made him immortal." Luke's smile was tinged with malice. "Is this about jealousy? You're jealous of the dead Cassius, who's now probably burning in hellfire? The deal depends on the terms. The kind of deal I... Luke made with the devil on your behalf is that I asked him to give you powers to help me." Ophelia's frustration boiled over. "One mistake, and we're dead. It just seems useless to help you." Luke's expression turned cold. "Fine. I'll ask the dark lord to take back what he gave you. And there's going to be hell to pay." Kael's intervention was swift. "No, no, no. Ophelia's kidding. We're going to help you." Luke's smile was a thin, cruel line.

The Throne Room, Selenea Realm. The Imperia's piercing gaze fell upon Maverick and Atticus as they stood before her. "Where have you been?" she asked, her voice like ice. Maverick hesitated, but Atticus's words cut her off. "The mortal realm, Mother. That's where we've been." The Imperia's expression turned stern. "You want me to strip you of your powers, so you can be mortal and…enjoy?" Atticus stepped forward, his tone apologetic. "No, Mother. We're sorry." Maverick's voice was laced with defiance. "I'm not sorry." Atticus's warning was swift. "Mave, don't disrespect our mother." Maverick's words spilled out in a rush. "She just asked us if we want to be powerless. But the great favorite daughter Odessa doesn't get asked that kind of question. She didn't listen to you. You told her to come home, but not once have you ever threatened to strip her powers. Yet, Atticus and I visit the mortal realm for a month, and you go mad on us." Atticus chimed in, his voice measured. "Mother, I'm afraid Mave is right. Odessa's been gone for years, and you didn't do anything about it…or her." The Imperia's silence was oppressive, her thoughts consumed by the truth in Maverick's words. Atticus and Maverick bowed, then turned to leave, abandoning her to her turbulent thoughts.

Back to the Mortal Realm. Calantha walked alone at night, her footsteps echoing through the deserted streets. Suddenly, a stranger appeared before her. "Hey," he said, his voice low and smooth. Calantha's gaze met his, and she replied, "Hey." — "I'm Eric McKenzie," he introduced himself. "And you are?" Calantha hesitated for a moment before responding, "I'm Calantha." Eric chuckled. "Just Calantha? No last name?" Calantha's cheeks flushed. "We just met, I don't…see…uhm, okay, I'm Calantha Singh." Eric's eyes sparkled. "Singh? That's beautiful." Their conversation was interrupted by a familiar voice. "Hey." Calantha forced a smile as Seth approached. "Can I talk to you…alone, perhaps?" he asked, his eyes narrowing at Eric. Calantha gestured to Eric. "I'm talking to this guy." Seth's expression turned cold. "Does he know what you are?

Or are you just going to use him like you used me?" Calantha's eyes flashed with defiance. "What? I didn't use you." Seth's voice dripped with sarcasm. "You didn't just hear that the four warlocks are in Emberdale, you knew our plan, and you wanted to get inside info by getting closer to me. You knew I wouldn't believe a thing, so you showed me proof that you're indeed a—" Calantha cut him off, her voice firm. "I used you, okay? So, what?" Eric's eyes widened in confusion. "What is he talking about?" Calantha turned to Eric. "Go. I'll see you if I happen to bump into you again. If you're attending Emberdale High, I'll see you there." Eric looked uncertain but nodded and left. Seth watched him go. "I believe you just met him." Calantha's tone was icy. "Not particularly your business, is it?" Seth chuckled, his eyes roaming over her. "No. Okay, I'm not mad that you used me. Why would I be mad? I mean, look at how beautiful you look." Calantha raised an eyebrow. "Am I supposed to say thank you or be impressed by your compliment?" Seth grinned. "Both, I believe."

Calantha's expression remained unyielding. "Well, I'm not grateful nor impressed." Seth's gaze lingered on her. "We could be together, a warlock and a witch." Calantha's response was firm. "I will never be with you, regardless of your warlock-ness, okay? Got that?" Seth's eyes narrowed. "You want to be with that mortal?"

Calantha's tone remained detached. "Still not particularly your business...uh...what's your name again?" Seth's smile was wry. "Seth." Calantha's eyes locked onto his. "Okay, Seth. Whether I want to be with that mortal or not, it isn't your business and will never be." Seth's gaze turned intense. "I think otherwise." Calantha's stomach began to ache, and she touched it instinctively. Seth's eyes widened in concern as he reached out to her. "Are you okay?" he asked. Calantha pulled away, her voice firm. "I'm fine." Seth's expression turned solicitous. "I can escort you back to your place." Calantha's response was curt. "Like I said, I'm fine. I can get myself home." Seth's eyes lingered on her, but before he could speak, Calantha vanished into thin air. "Lacunae magicae," she whispered, leaving Seth alone in the darkness.

22

CHAPTER XXII — Sisterly Concerns.

The Locker Room, Calantha sat with her sisters, Ayla and Odessa, in Emberdale High's ladies' locker room. Concern etched on their faces. "Calantha, are you okay? You didn't seem yourself last night," Ayla asked, her voice laced with worry. "My stomach was hurting," Calantha replied, her expression guarded. "You should see a doctor," Ayla suggested. Calantha's gaze flashed with defiance. "I'm a witch, I can cast a spell and be fine." Odessa's eyes narrowed. "Calantha, can I ask you something?" — "Go ahead." Calantha said. "Do you think redemption is possible for the darkest of souls?" Odessa's voice was laced with a mix of curiosity and concern. Calantha's brow furrowed. "What do you mean? Redemption for someone else or us?" Odessa's gaze locked onto hers. "Us. You, me, and Ayla. Do you think we can find redemption?" Calantha's expression turned cautious. "What makes you think my soul is the darkest or yours is?" Odessa's voice dropped to a whisper. "We used to hunt mortals, remember? Handing them over to the most evil man alive. Have you done worse without us?" Ayla chimed in, her voice firm. "Like changing paths, praying to the Dark Lord?" Calantha's eyes widened, caught off guard. "You know?" Ayla's gaze didn't waver. "We do, and you weren't planning to tell us, were you?" Calantha's defenses faltered. "I was." Odessa's expression turned stern. "What happened to the Triple Goddess?" Calantha's voice barely above a whisper. "They went silent on me… I was losing my powers." Odessa's eyes narrowed. "So, turning to Lucifer was the only option, what about Lilith or the Green Man?" Calantha's shoulders sagged. "I didn't think of them." Odessa's words cut deep. "Did you even think? Let's start there." Calantha's frustration boiled over. "Get off my case! You weren't losing powers, turning mortal. I did what I had to do." Ayla's voice sliced through the tension. "What did the Dark Lord get in return for your powers?" Calantha's response sent a chill through the air. "My soul, I believe." Odessa's eyes flashed with determination. "Your soul is still bound to the Triple Goddess. They didn't abandon you; they just went silent. Whatever Lucifer's getting, it's not your soul." Calantha's gaze faltered, uncertainty creeping in. Ayla's words pierced the silence. "Have you done anything evil since the Dark Lord's gifts?" Calantha's voice trembled. "I… killed three innocent mortal babies." Odessa's gasp echoed through the locker room. "You did what?"

Calantha's eyes pleaded for understanding. "It wasn't me; the Dark Lord controlled my body." Odessa's expression turned resolute. "You need to end your deal with the devil." Calantha's fear spiked. "I won't; I'll become powerless and vulnerable." Odessa's voice remained firm. "Sister, you've changed. You're killing mortals for the Dark Lord. This isn't who we are." Ayla's words reinforced Odessa's. "We stopped hunting mortals; now you're killing them for the Dark Lord. You're not yourself anymore." Calantha's desperation grew. "I can talk to him, the

Dark Lord, and negotiate a different payment." Odessa's eyes locked onto hers, filled with a mix of sadness and determination. "If Lucifer takes back his powers, you'll die and go to his realm. There you won't be his servant but yet another damned soul, tortured by his demons. He won't care. Listen to us, Sister. The Dark Lord is using you." Calantha's face twisted in anguish. "Since you think I'm evil, I shall leave at once. You wouldn't want to be near you or these mortals."

Ayla's voice called out, but Calantha was already gone, slamming the locker room door behind her.

As Calantha exited the locker room, she collided with a familiar figure - Eric. His bright smile faltered for a moment before he regained his composure. "Hey, watch where you're going," Eric teased, his eyes sparkling with amusement. Calantha's cheeks flushed. "Sorry, I wasn't paying attention. You go to this school too?"

Eric's eyes lit up. "Yeah, I do. I was going to tell you that the other day, but you kind of dismissed me." Calantha's expression turned sheepish. "Sorry about that." Eric's grin returned. "No worries. So, who was that guy? Your boyfriend?" Calantha's laughter was swift. "No, definitely not." Eric's eyes crinkled at the corners. "Well, then, can we grab a seat in the cafeteria together?" Calantha hesitated, her thoughts drifting to her sisters' warnings. But Eric's warm smile put her at ease. "Uh… my sisters won't really…uhm…you know what? Let's go."

As they strolled into the cafeteria, Calantha felt a sense of freedom she hadn't experienced in a long time. Their conversation flowed effortlessly, filled with laughter and jokes. For a fleeting moment, she forgot about the darkness lurking in her life.

Meanwhile, Ayla and Odessa emerged from the locker room, their expressions somber. As they passed by the cafeteria, they spotted Calantha laughing with Eric. Ayla's brow furrowed. "What is she doing with that mortal?" Odessa's gaze turned cold. "Probably doing Lucifer's bidding." Ayla's concern deepened. "Sister, we must stop her before it's too late." But Odessa's grip on her arm halted her. "No, Ayla. We've tried and failed. Everything has a price. Calantha will regret her choices when Lucifer's done with her." Ayla's eyes pleaded, but Odessa's resolve remained unshakeable. With a shared nod, they turned away, leaving Calantha to her mortal acquaintance. As they disappeared into the crowd, Calantha remained oblivious to the storm brewing around her. Her laughter and smiles were a temporary shield against the darkness closing in.

23

CHAPTER XXIII — Tangled Hearts and Twisted Magic.

A Day Later, Calantha sat on a fallen log in the woods, seeking solace amidst the chaos. Her thoughts were interrupted by Kael, Aria, and Ophelia. "Are you okay?" Ophelia asked, her tone laced with sarcasm. "It's not like you care," Calantha retorted. Ophelia smirked. "Revenge is what I want." Calantha's eyes flashed with defiance. "I'm more powerful than you." Ophelia sneered. "Oh, are you?" Kael and Aria chimed in, their voices in unison, "Immobilitas Absoluta, Statum Tenere!" Calantha froze, immobilized. "Let go of me," she demanded. Ophelia's eyes sparkled with curiosity. "Something's different about you. You're not as powerful as you were that day we fought."

Kael chimed in, "Maybe she's turning mortal too." Ophelia's gaze turned cold. "We need to kill her to find out." Calantha's eyes widened as Ophelia pulled out a knife. "Is this how it is now? Witches killing witches?" Ophelia corrected her, "We're not witches, not exactly. We know certain spells and have certain magic." Calantha's voice dripped with desperation. "Go ahead. Kill me. My life couldn't get any worse." Ophelia's smile faltered. "You were supposed to beg, and I'd show you no mercy." Calantha goaded her, "Or you just don't have it in you." Their standoff was interrupted by Eric who mistakenly stepped on something, watching from afar. Ophelia's gaze locked onto him, and she ordered Kael, "Go get him." Kael chased Eric deep into the woods. Eric stumbled, but before Kael could catch him, Seth appeared out of nowhere. Seth's presence startled Eric. "Seth? What are you doing here?" Kael asked. Seth's eyes narrowed. "I could ask you the same thing. And I won't let you kill him. He's mine." Kael hesitated. Seth grabbed Eric's hand and whispered, "Lacunae magicae."

They vanished, leaving Kael alone.

Seth and Eric reappeared at the basketball court. Eric gasped, disoriented. "What just happened? I was in the woods…"

Seth's voice soothed him. "Listen to my voice. Hear my words, and forget I said anything. Bless your mind, bless your heart, let these thoughts depart." Eric's eyes glazed over, his memories erased. "What are we doing here? Oh, I remember you." He said. "You wanted to tell me that the girl I saw you with told you to leave her alone." Seth said. "She did not do such." Eric said. Seth chuckled. "My bad then, move along, mortal." With that, Seth walked away, leaving Eric bewildered.

Kael returned to where Ophelia and Aria waited, his expression tense. "Where is he?" Aria asked, her eyes narrowing. "Seth took him," Kael replied, his voice laced with frustration. Ophelia's eyes snapped with anger. "What do you mean Seth took him?" Kael explained, "The mortal stumbled, and I was about to grab him, but Seth appeared out of nowhere." Ophelia's gaze turned calculating. "Does he know him or something?" Calantha, still immobilized, spoke up, "Yes, he does." Ophelia's attention shifted to Calantha. "How do you know that?" Calantha's smile hinted at secrets. "The person Seth took wants me, I believe he followed me here. Seth also wants me, and I think he followed me here too. Seth would kill him just because the poor mortal wants me." Ophelia's eyes flashed with curiosity. "Where is he taking him?" Calantha shrugged. "How am I supposed to know that?" Ophelia sneered. "You just acted omniscient a few seconds ago." Calantha's laughter sent a shiver down Ophelia's spine. "I think Seth will come for me soon, not violently, but to set me free and go after you. I don't think he knows you're making deals behind his back." Ophelia's face twisted in anger. "Seth isn't our leader. I am." Kael intervened, "I think we should let her go." Ophelia teased, "Why am I smelling feminine energy suddenly? Kael, are you turning soft? Oh, do forgive me, you were never hard." Aria chimed in, "Ophelia, please let's release her. If we want Odessa, we should go after her straight." Calantha chuckled, "Listen to them." Ophelia's gaze lingered on Calantha before she turned to Aria. "Remove your spell." The immobilizing spell lifted, and Calantha stood, her eyes never leaving Ophelia's. The trio departed, leaving Calantha to follow a few minutes later, her thoughts swirling with secrets and intentions.

Evening that day. Nicholas pulled up to Chloe's house, his heart racing with anticipation. He knocked on the door, and Chloe answered, her expression guarded. "Hey, Chloe," Nick said, his voice sincere. Chloe raised an eyebrow. "What do you want, Nick?"

Nick took a deep breath. "To apologize, the right way." Chloe's gaze softened, and she stepped aside. "Okay, come in." They sat down in the cozy living room, the tension between them palpable. Nick's eyes locked onto Chloe's, his voice filled with emotion.

"Look, I'm truly sorry for always seeing you as my second option. I'll always regret that. But Chloe… I realize now that I love you, and I always will." Chloe's expression remained still, her thoughts hidden. Nick continued, his words spilling out. "Ayla and I are done, for good. And to be honest, she's… different. She's a witch."

Chloe's eyebrows shot up, a chuckle escaping her lips. "A witch? Is that a joke?" Nick's face turned serious, before a mischievous grin spread across his face. "No, I'm serious… just kidding! You know jokes are my thing." Chloe's laughter faded, replaced by a gentle smile. "I still love you too, Nick." Nick's heart skipped a beat. "So, we can get back together?" Chloe's nod was hesitant. "Yes, but we need to take things slow." Nick's face lit up. "Fast or slow, I'm all in." Their smiles met, and the space between them seemed to dissolve. The evening's reconciliation had begun, filled with promise and renewed love.

24

CHAPTER XXIV — The Gathering Storm.

Two weeks had passed since Calantha, the witch, vanished into thin air. Her sisters, Odessa and Ayla, sat in their apartment, worry etched on their faces. "Do you think Calantha will come back?" Ayla asked, her voice laced with concern. Odessa's expression was grim. "I don't know. She's nowhere to be found. I think it's time we ask for help." Ayla's eyes narrowed. "Who's on your mind?" Odessa hesitated before responding, "My mother." Ayla's eyes widened. "The Imperia?" Odessa nodded, her jaw set. "She's the only one who can help us." With a deep breath, Odessa stepped back from Ayla and closed her eyes. She inhaled and exhaled slowly, focusing her energy. The air around her began to shimmer, and her mother, The Imperia, materialized before them.

The Imperia's piercing gaze swept the room, her presence commanding attention. "What do you want?" she asked, her voice firm but laced with a hint of warmth. Odessa approached her mother, her eyes locked on hers. "Hello, Mother. We need your help. Calantha's gone missing, and we can't find her." The Imperia's expression softened slightly. "I'll find her for you," she said, her voice dripping with an otherworldly authority. Odessa's relief was palpable. "Thank you, Mother." The Imperia's gaze turned serious. "I was going to come here even if you didn't call for me. Something's coming, something that threatens this mortal realm."

Odessa's curiosity was piqued. "What's coming?" The Imperia's words sent a shiver down Odessa's spine. "Sanity-Shattering Beings and The Unholy Horde." Ayla's eyes widened in horror. "Sanity-Shattering? Are we all going to go crazy?" The Imperia's expression was grim. "Only the mortals." Odessa's mind reeled. "What's the Unholy Horde?" The Imperia's voice was laced with a hint of disgust. "A group of evil entities, an army of demonic beings." Odessa's eyes narrowed. "Lucifer's behind this, isn't he?"

The Imperia nodded. "He is." Ayla's voice trembled. "So, which one is coming first?" The Imperia's expression was uncertain. "That, I don't know. We must stay prepared." Just then, Maverick appeared out of nowhere, her presence as sudden as a storm. "Sanity-Shattering Beings are coming first," she said, her voice dripping with an otherworldly confidence. The Imperia's gaze turned piercing. "When did you arrive here?" Maverick's smile was enigmatic. "Millenia ago." Odessa's eyes narrowed. "So, you heard what Mom said?" Maverick's gaze locked onto Odessa. "Yes, the Unholy Horde." Odessa's expression turned serious. "Why are you here?" Maverick's smile grew wider. "To help, of course." The Imperia's gaze swept the room, her expression a mix of approval and wariness. "We need all the help we can get." With Maverick's arrival, the room seemed to vibrate with an otherworldly energy. The air was thick with anticipation, and the sisters knew that their world was about to change forever.

Lucifer, the Prince of Darkness, sat upon his throne, his piercing gaze surveying the depths of the infernal realm. Beside him, Lilith, the Queen of the Night, watched with an air of trepidation. "The mortal realm will soon be mine to conquer," Lucifer declared, his voice like thunder in the underworld. "With my demonic army, I shall invade it, and all flesh will die." Lilith's eyes narrowed, her voice laced with caution. "Isn't that a bit too much, my lord? The mortal realm is not ours to claim." Lucifer's expression turned cold, his eyes flashing with anger. "Lilith, this will happen whether you approve or not. I am the King of Hell, the Prince of Darkness. My will shall not be questioned." Lilith's gaze fell, her voice barely above a whisper. "What about the witches who praise you, my lord? Are they to meet their demise alongside the mortals?" Lucifer's chuckle sent shivers through the underworld. "No, Lilith. Only those who rejected me shall suffer my wrath. Those who have sworn allegiance to me shall be spared... for now." The air grew thick with tension as Lilith nodded, her eyes never leaving Lucifer's face. The Prince of Darkness leaned forward, his voice taking on a sinister tone. "The time of reckoning approaches, Lilith. Prepare the demonic horde. We shall march upon the mortal realm, and none shall stand in our way." As Lucifer's words faded into the darkness, the underworld trembled with anticipation. The infernal realm stirred, its inhabitants sensing the approaching storm. The mortal realm, once a distant concern, now stood on the brink of annihilation.

The next day, The Imperia ventured into the woods, her determined stride carrying her toward the clearing where

Calantha lay sleeping. As she approached, Calantha stirred, her eyes fluttering open. "Do you remember me?" The Imperia asked, her voice gentle. Calantha's gaze cleared, and she smiled weakly. "Of course. You're Odessa's mother." The Imperia's expression softened. "They're worried about you, Calantha. I think you should come with me." Calantha's brow furrowed. "They're…?" The Imperia's eyes locked onto Calantha's. "Odessa and Ayla. They've been searching for you everywhere. Odessa called for me, asking for my help to find you. That's how much she cares for you, Calantha." Calantha's expression changed, a mix of emotions swirling in her eyes. "I wasn't on good terms with them when I left," she said, her voice barely above a whisper. The Imperia's voice was laced with understanding. "I know. But they want to help you, Calantha. They want you back." Calantha nodded, a resolve forming on her face. "I'll come with you." The Imperia smiled, her eyes warm with relief. She joined Calantha on a fallen log, and they sat together in comfortable silence for a moment. "Calantha, there's something you need to know," The Imperia said, her voice serious. "Something's coming, something that threatens your realm." Calantha's gaze turned intense. "What is it?" The Imperia's words painted a grim picture. "Sanity-Shattering Beings and the Unholy Horde. They'll bring destruction and chaos to your realm." Calantha's eyes widened, her face pale. "I've made a deal with the devil," she whispered, her voice trembling. The Imperia's expression turned thoughtful. "I understand, Calantha. I know what it's like to make difficult choices." Calantha's gaze locked onto The Imperia's, and for a moment, they shared a deep understanding. "We should leave," The Imperia said, standing up. "We have much to prepare for." Calantha nodded, and together, they vanished into the trees, ready to face the impending storm.

25

CHAPTER XXV — Beyond the Veil of Sanity, Pt. 1

A week had passed, and Thursday's warm sunlight streamed through the cafeteria's windows. Calantha, Ayla and Odessa sat together, their conversation flowing effortlessly. "Do you guys think we're prepared?" Odessa asked, her brow furrowed with concern. Ayla's confident smile reassured her. "We're the daughters of darkness, not that dark, though. I think we're prepared." Their discussion was interrupted by Jamie Scratch's approach. "Hey, guys," he said, his eyes sparkling with excitement. Odessa raised an eyebrow. "Mr. Scratch. What do you want this time around?" Jamie's grin widened. "Haven't you heard about the festival happening tomorrow?" Ayla's curiosity piqued. "No. Where is it happening, and who's hosting it?" Jamie shrugged. "I didn't care enough to research the details. All I know is it's going to be lit. Since Nicholas and Chloe are back together, I figured he wouldn't invite you, so I'm inviting you instead." Ayla's eyes narrowed. "Nicholas and Chloe are doing what now?" Odessa and Calantha chimed in unison, "Sister?" Ayla feigned innocence. "What? The question

101

was innocent." Jamie handed Odessa a colorful poster. "So, are you coming?" Odessa took the poster, her eyes scanning the vibrant design. "Yes, we're in." As Jamie departed, the sisters exchanged knowing glances. The Luminaria Festival's promise of music, food and joy seemed like the perfect distraction from their dark realities. Little did they know, the shadows were stirring, awaiting their chance to strike.

Ayla's eyes scanned the poster, her brow furrowing as she read the words "Abaddon Arts" emblazoned across the top. "Abaddon Arts?" she asked, her voice laced with concern. Calantha leaned in, curiosity etched on her face. "What's that?" Ayla's gaze met Odessa's, a silent understanding passing between them. "An organization hosting the festival," Ayla replied, her tone measured.

Odessa's eyes narrowed. "Abaddon means destruction… These Sanity-Shattering Beings are disguising themselves as festival hosters?" Calantha's expression turned grim. "And everyone will be there. This feels like a horror movie we're about to walk into." Ayla's voice was laced with urgency. "What do we do?" Odessa's eyes sparkled with a plan. "Let's discourage them from going."

Calantha nodded. "Clever." The trio rose, determination etched on their faces, and approached Nicholas and Chloe. "Hey, Nicky and Chloe," Odessa said, her tone light. Nicholas and Chloe turned, their faces a picture of blissful ignorance. "Hey," they chimed in unison. Odessa's smile was radiant. "You two look beautiful together. Right, Ayla?" Ayla's agreement was enthusiastic. "Yes, you two look amazing." Chloe's response was tinged with awkwardness. "Thank you, I guess." Odessa's expression turned serious. "We've heard about tomorrow's festival. We think it's not safe to go." Chloe's laughter was dismissive. "What? Ayla's going to do some magic on us? Apparently, she's a witch." Ayla's eyes flashed with annoyance. "I'm not a witch. Where did you hear that?" Chloe's shrug was nonchalant. "People talk, Ayla." Odessa's gaze pinned Nicholas. "I don't think it's people who talk, Nicholas. You talk, and you said some absurd things." Nicholas's face darkened. "Can you all please leave?" The sisters exchanged knowing glances before turning to depart. As they returned to their seats in the cafeteria, Odessa's voice was laced with concern. "I don't think this will work." Calantha's nod was somber. "Yeah, it won't."

A day later. The sun dipped below Emberdale's horizon, casting a warm orange glow over the Luminaria Festival. Laughter and music filled the air as warlocks, cult members, Nicholas and his friends, and the three sisters, Odessa, Ayla and Calantha, mingled with the Imperia and Maverick. Joy was palpable, until the festival's hosters, clad in black glasses, ascended the stage. A hush fell over the crowd as the Sanity-Shattering Beings revealed themselves. One being's voice echoed through the silence, "Behold, ladies and gentlemen. We give you the gift of the night. Enjoy and indulge." As the Beings removed their glasses, their piercing gazes met the crowd. Pandemonium erupted. Uncontrollable laughter consumed the masses, except for Odessa, Ayla, Calantha, Maverick, the Imperia, Luke, Wystan, Seth and Silas. Odessa's concern was palpable. "What's happening? Why is everyone laughing?" The Imperia's voice was laced with foreboding. "The shattering has taken effect." The Sanity-Shattering Beings focused on Odessa's group, their heads twitching left to right, attempting to shatter their sanity. But they failed. With a sudden vanish, the Beings disappeared, leaving behind a sea of madness. Luke approached Odessa, his expression uneasy. "What's going on?" Odessa's tone was wary. "Why ask me? We're not friends. We fought a life-threatening battle." Luke's urgency overrode his animosity. "Trust me, I hate you for that, but this isn't normal. Why aren't they stopping?" Odessa's explanation was grim. "They're insane. Those beings made every mortal mad." Luke's determination surprised Odessa. "How do we stop them?" The Imperia's skepticism was evident. "Why stop them? You wanted mortals dead. They're crazy now, half congratulations." Luke's conviction was unwavering. "I still want them dead, but I'd rather kill them than let something make them crazy." Calantha's incredulity was palpable. "This is huge, and you're thinking about killing them?" Luke's resolve faltered. "Okay, no killing then." In the midst of chaos, unlikely alliances were forged.

The group converged on the school hall, seeking space to strategize amidst the chaos engulfing Emberdale. Luke's concern was palpable. "What's our next move? The entire town's lost its mind!" Calantha's determination shone through. "Can't we just find and kill it?" Imperia's wisdom tempered their zeal. "These Eldritch horrors defy mortal comprehension. Physical destruction is impossible. Our only hope lies in banishment." Luke's curiosity got the better of him. "But how?" Just then, a stranger entered the hall. "I know how to end these Eldritch horrors," he declared. Odessa's caution was warranted. "Who are you?" The newcomer approached. "I'm Thorold Thorne, from the Arcania realm." Ayla's curiosity was piqued. "What brings you here?" Thorold's offer was genuine. "You need help, don't you? I'm here to assist, unless you'd rather I left." Odessa's interest deepened. "What do you know about these horrors?" Thorold's expression turned grim. "In Arcania, we've faced similar terrors. This is merely the beginning. The madness will intensify." Imperia's concern was evident. "What comes next?" Thorold's words painted a dire picture. "Echoes of the past will haunt the victims. Painful memories and traumas will resurface, distorted reality. They'll struggle to distinguish past from present." Seth's question echoed the group's dread. "Is this hell?" Thorold's affirmation was solemn. "Literally." Odessa's determination rallied the group. "How can we stop it?"

Thorold's knowledge offered a glimmer of hope. "We can brew the Elixir of Sanity. It requires wolf's bane and starlight bloom. This potion will restore clarity, reality, and rational thinking, buying time to devise a more permanent solution." With newfound purpose, the group dispersed to gather ingredients. Under the light of a full moon, Imperia invoked the lunar energy. "Moonlight, full and perfect, descend upon us." As they steeped the ingredients in a silver cauldron, the group channeled magical energy. In unison, they recited the ancient incantation:

"Moonlight, descend within me! Silver star, total infusion! Selene's essence, flow within. Exceptional fire, ignite within! Magical power, rise and grow! Aqueonia's flow, grant vitality! Earth's balance, stabilize this potion! My shield, total protection! Moon's seal, seal this magic! Air, fire, water, earth, I conjure! Elements, balance and harmony! Nature's rhythm, attune within! Darkness flees, Xylara's power! Thorne's thorn, protection's spine! Eldrid's essence, wisdom's guide!"

As the incantation faded, reality reasserted itself. The group's chanting gave way to jubilation, their bond strengthened by their shared triumph.

26

CHAPTER XXVI — Beyond the Veil of Sanity, Pt. 2

The next day, the Sanity-Shattering Beings reconvened at the Luminaria lake, site of the ill-fated festival. With sinister intent, they invoked the next horror: "Echoes of the Past." Their incantation echoed through the air:

"By the shadows of the past, I summon thy pain.
  Forgetfulness, dispelled, memories arise.
  Darkness of mind, open thine eyes.
  Echoes of torment, ignite within.
  Rise again, rise again, all horrors of yesterday.
  Unleash the abyss, shatter the mind, and let madness reign."

Pandemonium erupted as Emberdale's mortals succumbed to their resurfaced traumas. Screams and wails filled the air, echoing through every corner of the town. The group, now leaderless without Thorold, gathered in desperation. They joined hands, seeking solace in their shared plight, and called upon Hecate:

"Hecate, Goddess of Shadows, hear our call.
Free the minds of Emberdale, one and all.
Lift the veil of madness, bring clarity's light.
Restore sanity to mortals, in this dark night.
Drive away the echoes, of painful past.
Grant peace to troubled minds, and make them last.
By your power, Hecate, we beg of thee.
Free Emberdale's people, from insanity."

Their pleas hung in the air, but the Sanity-Shattering Beings would not relent. They summoned the third horror: "Self-mutilation" their voices dripping with malice:

"Khthonic powers, ascend within.
Unholy flesh, now rend and spin.
Carnifex, arise, and claim thy due.
Self-mutilation's horrors, we invoke anew."

Emberdale's people, consumed by madness, turned against themselves. Self-inflicted wounds and screams of agony filled the air. The group, horrified, chanted once more:

"Hecate, Goddess of Shadows, hear our plea.
Shield Emberdale from Self-mutilation's spree.
Grant its people strength, to resist the urge.
Preserve their minds, and soothe their purge."

As the last words faded, an unsettling silence fell. The horrors ceased, and the Sanity-Shattering Beings vanished, never to return. Emberdale, scarred but spared, slowly began to heal. The group, exhausted but resilient, shared a glimmer of hope.

Hecate's power had saved them, but at what cost? The memories of that terrible day would haunt them forever.

CHAPTER XXVII — The Unholy Horde.

Two weeks of uneasy calm had passed in Emberdale.

The townspeople had returned to their daily lives, oblivious to the horrors they had faced. Luke and his warlocks had resumed their hostility towards Odessa and her people. Odessa, Ayla, Calantha, Maverick, and the Imperia gathered in Odessa's apartment, discussing their next move. "Now we should expect demons?" Odessa asked. The Imperia nodded. "Yes." — "Are we going to physically fight them?" Calantha inquired.

The Imperia turned to Calantha. "As a witch, you know of the spell to summon the void. We can offer the demons to the void." — "That's genius," Ayla said. "Lucifer won't see it coming."

Meanwhile, in the Infernal Realm, Lucifer addressed his demonic army. "Invade the mortal realm. Kill everyone in your path."

The army vanished from Hell and reappeared in Emberdale, casting a dark cloud over the town. Odessa and her allies rushed outside to investigate. The demonic army began slaughtering mortals. Calantha searched for the spell as the cult's members fell, except Luke and his warlocks, who joined Odessa's group.

Calantha found the spell and chanted:

"Zhrakkor, void of eternal darkness, hear our plea,
Consume this demonic horde, set mortals free.
Eat their darkness, drink their pain,
Spare the innocent, void, we pray in vain.
Devour their evil, swallow their might,
Leave no remnant, of their wicked sight.
Cleanse this realm, with thy dark hunger's sway,
Protect the innocent, void, come what may."

The void appeared, devouring the demonic entities. The group parted ways.

Luke and his warlocks met the Dark Lord at their hideout.

"My lord," they said. The Dark Lord cursed them:

"I curse you, warlocks, with mortal fate,
Stripped of powers, forever to wait.
To walk on Earth, alone, unknown.
You shall age, weaken, as mortals do,
Know strife, sickness, disease, and pain anew.
Grievous guilt shall haunt your every breath,
Longing for death, but never to find rest.
Your days shall stretch, an endless, painful road,
No respite, no peace, forever to atone.
May your mortal form betray your wicked past,
And may your heart forever be tormented at last."

The Dark Lord vanished.

Calantha sought solace in the woods but was interrupted by the Dark Lord. "My lord," she said.

The Dark Lord repeated the curse, condemning her to mortal

fate.

Calantha's eyes widened as the Dark Lord disappeared.

CHAPTER XXVIII — Sisters United: the Final Act.

Weeks had passed since the battle against the Eldritch horrors and the Dark Lord. Calantha kept her newfound mortality a secret from her sisters, fearing they would worry and opt to stay in Emberdale. The Imperia, Odessa, and Maverick sat in the apartment, preparing to leave.

"We must return home," the Imperia said. "The fight is done," Odessa agreed. "We've defeated the horrors, the Dark Lord, and Cassius." — "What about your life here?" Maverick asked. Odessa smiled. "I've protected these mortals. It's time to leave." — "Goodbye, sisters," Odessa said, embracing Ayla and Calantha. As they departed for the Selenea realm, Ayla and Calantha remained in the apartment. "I need to tell you something," Calantha said, her voice barely above a whisper. Ayla's eyes narrowed. "What is it?"

Calantha took a deep breath. "The Dark Lord took back his gifts. I'm mortal now, powerless." Ayla's eyes widened. "Why didn't you tell Odessa?" Calantha shrugged. "She would have worried and stayed. Sometimes, we need to move on without our families." Ayla's expression turned somber. "I don't have a family."

The room fell silent.

Meanwhile, the four warlocks, now mortal and powerless, left Emberdale. The town began to flourish, free from the shadows of darkness. Nicholas and Chloe's relationship blossomed, while Austin fell for Zara Smith. Jasmine and Eric started hanging out.

Two months passed. Maverick returned to the mortal realm, seeking Ayla and Calantha. "It's time to join your sister in Selenea," Maverick said. Ayla and Calantha agreed, eager to reunite with Odessa.

In the Selenea realm, Odessa's eyes lit up as she saw her sisters and Maverick. "What brings you here?" Odessa asked.

Maverick smiled. "I thought you could use your sisters. They're the only ones you'd literally kill for." Odessa's face softened, and she hugged Ayla and Calantha tightly. The Imperia watched, a warm smile on her face. The sisters were together again, ready to face new challenges and forge a brighter future.

About the Author

Sello S. Makhafola is an aspiring author with a passion for storytelling. Born and raised in Mokopane, Extension 19, he developed a love for writing at an early age. With a unique voice and perspective, Sello brings a fresh take to the fantasy/mystery genre.

His writing journey began with writing short stories just for fun.

When not writing, Sello enjoys sketching, reading, making music, and can often be found watching series.

You can connect with me on:

f https://www.facebook.com/s3llomakhafola?mibextid=ZbWKwL

https://bsky.app/profile/s3llo.bsky.social

9 7 9 8 2 3 0 6 9 8 5 9 3